Gary was born in the village of Bendooragh, near Ballymoney in north Antrim. Growing up in the 1970s, he used to listen to the stories told by his grandfather and a group of his friends who met frequently in his home. As time passed, the memory of these stories faded but not his memory of how enjoyable they were to hear. The aim of this book is to bring laughs and happiness to the reader in the old tradition of storytelling that has been largely eclipsed by modernity.

This book is dedicated to the memory of my grandfather, Archie Atcheson, and his generation of storytellers who made their own entertainment before the advent of multimedia and reliance on television for fun and laughter.

Gary Blair

TALL SHORT TALES

Yarns from Northern Ireland

AUSTIN MACAULEY PUBLISHERS™

LONDON • CAMBRIDGE • NEW YORK • SHARJAH

A CIP catalogue record for this title is available from the British Library.

ISBN 9781528988988 (Paperback)
ISBN 9781528988995 (ePub e-book)

www.austinmacauley.com

First Published (2020)
Austin Macauley Publishers Ltd
25 Canada Square
Canary Wharf
London
E14 5LQ

I would like to acknowledge the help and support I received from my immediate family and the 'Blues Brothers' who encouraged me and took a genuine and avid interest in my work and ideas.

Working Class Hero

A chink of light cut its way through a narrow slit, where the curtains met, and attacked the sleeping eyes of John Spence. He opened one eye to challenge the intrusion and quickly closed it again. Although awake, John resisted the urge to get up and greet the morning – if it was indeed morning for it could be much later. He shut his eyes tightly, in a bid to return to the tranquillity of a dreamless sleep but the light had done its work. Like it or not, John was awake and left with no choice but to face the day ahead.

Downstairs in the living room of the two-up, two-down terraced house, Madge Spence sat, gloomily clutching a mug of tea with both hands as if to let go would mean the mug would escape. She scanned the room, acknowledging the frayed curtains, the ancient television and the scuffed armchair and sofa. Madge was a woman who went through the daily trial of coming to terms with her lot in life. Every morning, she would get up, make a pot of tea, and sit in the same uncomfortable wooden chair sipping her hot, sweet tea, and deliberate on how cruel her life had been. It had all began so promising. On leaving school, she got a job in the shirt factory and met the man who would one day be her husband. Their courtship was a whirlwind of nights out and long walks on a Sunday. He had boasted of the money he would make, and she confided that she would continue to work in the shirt factory regardless how rich they would become.

The wedding was a small affair, in a local church that neither groom nor bride had attended with much enthusiasm or regularity. Afterwards, they had a reception in a local bar and headed off for two days to Donaghadee. They would have gone further, but with Madge being already three months pregnant, her new husband, Ronnie, said it would be far too dangerous. Anyway, they would get a foreign holiday after the child was born, he promised. After three testing months, living in her cramped mother's house, Madge successfully secured them a marital home nearby. He would have taken care of all that, Ronnie had said, but he was far too busy earning money and caring for his beloved pigeons, who were still living in a loft, in the back yard of his father's home.

Madge reflected bitterly, how they had scraped together enough money to buy a strange assortment of second hand furniture. The new stuff would come, Ronnie assured her, but this would get them started. He would be getting a promotion for sure, and as soon as the baby came, everything would improve. At that point, Madge slowly removed her hands from the mug and placed one over each eye. The furniture around and below her was the exact same furniture, they had bought all those years ago!

Eighteen years ago, in fact, she thought with renewed anger! Slowly, she opened her fingers and looked again at the furnishings, as if they might have changed their appearance and become new and fresh. She sighed deeply as she recognised the same old tatty chairs and scuffed linoleum. Removing her hands from her face, Madge pulled a ridiculously long cigarette from the pack beside her mug of now lukewarm tea and lit it, inhaling and exhaling deeply.

What a life! What a house!

A slight noise distracted Madge from her melancholy and she turned her head slightly to glance out the kitchen window. Ronnie Spence, oblivious to his wife's rage and resentment, and unaware of her piercing looks through the glass, held his favourite pigeon lovingly in his hands. Although she couldn't hear what he was saying, Madge shook her head in despair and disbelief.

Out there talking to a bird! He never says a word to me, he wouldn't make a bed or brush the floor yet there he is, out there making small talk with a pigeon! Still shaking her head, she watched as Ronnie smiled fondly at the disinterested bird and uttered a few more words of love and encouragement.

What a man! What a waste!

Suddenly, Madge was distracted from the sight of her introverted husband and his pigeon. A creaking noise from above alerted her to the imminent arrival of her useless, lazy son. *It's fine for him to lie in his bed until this time of the day! He has not a care in the world!* She glanced again at her husband, who had now set the pigeon on a narrow shelf, and seemed to be talking more earnestly to it. *The apple didn't fall far from the tree*, she thought bitterly. *Well, at least he worked for a while*, she reasoned, looking again at her husband, who was now looking at the sky. *That useless cretin up there has yet to start*, she mused looking towards the ceiling.

What an excuse for a son! What a lazy lump!

The door opened slowly and noisily, and John stumbled into the packed living room. Silently, he moved towards the chair, pausing to help himself to one of Madge's cigarettes. He lit it and sat down heavily as if the exertion had been unreasonable and extreme. Madge marvelled that he had accomplished the walk from his bed to the chair, with one eye half opened and the other tightly shut. Even the extraction of the cigarette had been done without the aid of vision. She looked at him wondering if he had fallen asleep again as both his eyes closed. Madge had never known what to do with John's hair. As a child, the barber seemed every bit as bewildered. It was as if John's hair had a mind of its own and today was no exception. Madge sighed again and looked fiercely at her son. *Skin and bones*, she thought. *All hair and ribs!*

"Any tea in that pot, Ma?" John drawled quietly.

Madge reached over to the nearby unit and retrieved a mug, slamming it down angrily on the table. She used to be a trim 8 stones but was now just over fifteen, which didn't work well with her 5'2" height. Her weight fought against her every movement but she did not blame herself for it. After fifteen years in the shirt factory, the business ran into trouble and closed its doors to the world, leaving Madge and Ronnie unemployed and unemployable. She could never explain her refusal to work somewhere else, rather she just accepted that her working life ended the day the machines shut down for the last time. Ronnie had worked for short periods in various jobs, but he had either been sacked for bad time keeping or had found a reason for leaving. Now they lived in a terraced bubble, where time ended and began again on their front door step.

John opened his eyes warily, needing an ashtray but too afraid to ask for one. He tapped his ash into his hand and looked at his mother. *She has had that bathrobe for as long as I remember*, he mused thoughtfully. *And them rollers in her hair! Every morning in life, she sat there drinking her tea and coughing, making the rollers bob forward and backwards.*

"That for me, is it?" he asked, nodding to the mug of black tea.

"Aye, and if you can find the energy, there's milk in the fridge and sugar in the larder!" Madge barked back. "And there's a letter for you there, if you're interested," she continued, nodding at a brown envelope on the table.

John sat up in surprise. He was not someone who was accustomed to getting mail. Gingerly, he reached across and gently took the envelope from off the table and examined it closely. He lifted a nearby biro and slid it along the top of the envelope as if it was something of immense value, and deserved to be handled with care and respect. Madge stared at him impatiently.

"Just open the thing!" she yelled "You're as bad as your da! Everything has to be a drama with you both! I don't know what you're being so canny about, 'cause it's from the broo. It says so on the front at the postmark!"

Suddenly, both of John's eyes were wide open as he quickly completed the task of opening the envelope, and tore out the item contained therein. A letter and…a giro!

He scanned the letter, and took in nothing of the content and diverted his eyes instead to the giro. If it were possible for his eyes to open any wider, they would have done so. It was a cheque for £260.83!

"How much?" Madge asked, hoping for a percentage of it.

Silently, John handed her the letter but held on to the giro, studying it as an art lover would study the Mona Lisa. Madge read the letter carefully. It was a cheque for money, the Social Security Office owed John. He had been in receipt of under payments but this had now been rectified, and the enclosed giro cheque was the amount owing.

As if the armchair had suddenly caught fire, John leapt up and ran towards the door. The half-smoked cigarette balanced precariously on the edge of the table, and the mug of black tea sat neglected on the table.

"Where are you for in such a hurry?" she demanded.

"Away up to get on me!" John shouted back, already half way up the stairs.

The back door opened, letting in a blast of cold air that nipped at Madge's feet. A slam and the heat returned. Madge looked up to see Ronnie looking at her with what might pass as interest.

"What's all the noise about?" he asked timidly.

"I'm pregnant!" Madge answered sarcastically. "Just found out there now."

"Any tea left in that pot?" Ronnie enquired as if his wife hadn't spoken a word.

Madge looked at Ronnie, then the teapot and then lit another cigarette.

What an idiot, she thought. *And what an idiot son!*

The post office was busy for a Saturday morning. Not exceptionally full of people but busy nonetheless for the sole teller, Joan Grace. This is not how Joan had intended to spend her Saturday morning. Indeed, working as a post office cashier wasn't how Joan intended to spend her working life. She looked glumly at the queue of people formed before her, wishing it was time for her tea break. There was a colleague out in the back office but he must have fallen asleep as he had 'nipped out' an hour ago, and hadn't come back.

As she waited for Mrs Freeman to find whatever she was looking for in her over-packed handbag, Joan reflected on her life. She remembered the flush of joy she had felt when she had been accepted into Queens University! The pride of her beaming parents and the endless calls her mother made to neighbours and distant relatives, relishing in this opportunity to boast about the intelligence of her daughter! She recalled with less enthusiasm her first encounter with Philip Bates, sporting all-rounder and dressed like a bit player from Miami Vice. She wistfully relived that night at the disco when he arrived with bleached hair, a white suit, turquoise T-shirt and no socks. Well, it was 1984 she told herself.

That first date led to a whirlwind romance and ended up in a marriage that lasted a full two years. She soon discovered that Mr Philip Bates was a womaniser and incompetent. Oh yes, he could interview well with his boyish charm and even white teeth but that was about it. Underneath all the shiny veneer, there was nothing of substance. They'd had three foreign holidays that first year, and it didn't strike Joan as odd that she had to pay the full price for two of them. He was just getting on his feet and it wasn't easy to get the right job without a degree (Philip had discovered that his charm was worth nothing to an impassive examination paper). Yes, surely he had talked himself into some good jobs but the problem was that he seemed to have the uncanny ability to talk himself back out of them again.

She reflected with mixed feelings that Sunday morning, when he had 'nipped out' to get milk and a newspaper. He had spent the previous day taking boxes and bags of outdated clothing to a charity shop, whilst she had manned the cash desk at the sub post office, where she had been forced to take employment out of need. He had been away an hour when Joan decided to leave her bed and have a black coffee and read the teletext. Another hour passed. Then another…

It was teatime when she found the note. She had decided to break the monotony by changing the bedclothes and there it was, in an envelope addressed to her. It was an eloquently written epistle, she thought bitterly. Grammatically correct and with excellent punctuation and many impressive metaphors. What it all boiled down to was that he was gone. Her marriage was over.

Joan remembered feeling remarkably calm. She folded the letter, placed it back in the envelope and threw it on top of the wardrobe. She then proceeded to change the bedding and fetched a bag from the kitchen into which she swept his remaining after shaves and whatever clothes he had forgotten to take. Then, despite herself, she laughed! *Of course, he was moving on! All that nonsense about the Charity Shop? Not even a Charity Shop would have taken those ridiculous outfits! Philip had reached 1986 and stopped!* She then thought about his toupee and how he believed no one knew...and Joan Grace laughed, and laughed and laughed...

"I know, I have it here somewhere," muttered the ancient Mrs Freeman, as she rummaged through her handbag.

The exclamation brought Joan back sharply to the post office counter, where she sat awaiting the discovery of Mrs Freeman's electric bill. She watched with growing exasperation as Mrs Freeman proceeded to remove every obstacle to finding the elusive bill. At least three paper tissues were set on the counter, one with lipstick on it and another with an unidentifiable mess. As if feeling the need to explain the object, Mrs Freeman paused in her search and looked at Joan Grace.

"It's a biscuit. I go to a wee meeting for folk my age and they give us biscuits. Because I am hard of hearing, I never know what they're saying so I just nod, you see? Then they give me biscuits I don't like, so they do. Well, I can hardly give them back after me nodding my head and all, so I wrap them in tissue paper and stick them in my bag, you see," she said pointing at the mess on the counter. Joan wrinkled her forehead to indicate that she did indeed see, and then nodded at the bulging handbag in a bid to encourage Mrs Freeman to resume her search. Mrs Freeman scowled, annoyed that this jumped-up cashier had no interest in her story about the biscuit. After a few moments, she pulled out a packet of tablets and stared intently at them.

"Oh, I don't believe it!" she exclaimed loudly. "My blood pressure tablets! Do you know, I have searched high and low for these and couldn't think where I'd put them and they were in here the whole time!"

She grinned happily at Joan, who rolled her eyes and wished for this morning to be over.

Alfie Watters was also becoming impatient. He had a letter to post, recorded delivery, and it was vital that he would accomplish this task immediately. Alfie knew he wasn't like other people. They all led dull lives and that would have been Alfie's fate too had he not been blessed with an amazing imagination. In a bid to escape the financial hardship and mundane existence he had been allotted, he learned as a child how to live an alternative, imaginary life where Alfie Watters was a man of significance!

Alfie had not enjoyed school but he did develop an almost unhealthy interest in history. Indeed, his fascination with dashing figures, powerful kings and emperors, decorated generals and homicidal despots had caused his teachers and his parents no small amount of concern. As Alfie listened to the accounts of their lives, he couldn't stop himself *becoming* one of them. Whilst all of this remained in his mind, it didn't matter to everyone else but when he raced to the playground at breaks and on the way home from school, the disturbing reality of Alfie's daydreams took on a new twist!

Docile dogs became wolves, cars became tanks and cats were suddenly wild tigers! Alfie saw all these things, things no one else could see. The aging lollipop man was an agent from the former Eastern Bloc who used his position to hear snippets of information from careless children. So convinced was Alfie about this, he always crossed the roads a safe distance from the lollipop man and always smirked triumphantly at him as if he had won a victory of some kind. Alfie admired the apparent disinterest and nonchalance of the lollipop man who never responded to Alfie's behaviour. To Alfie, this only served to prove how effective a spy the lollipop man really was...

On leaving school, Alfie became more and more introverted. He took to spending most of his time in his bedroom, watching historical films and imagining himself to be a part of them. Then he would spend hours reconstructing the film and placing himself firmly in it, playing a central role. Alfie then became frustrated as he convinced himself that his version of the film was much better than the Hollywood version yet his would never be screened.

Eventually, his concerned mother acted. She was convinced that Northern Ireland was no place for one as easily influenced as Alfie so she contacted her brother in Doncaster and asked if he could take Alfie over there and get him a job. Her brother obliged and Alfie set off on a new adventure. At Belfast International Airport, he saw spies and assassins everywhere. Aboard the plane, he managed to terrify himself imagining the elderly couple opposite him were hijackers. Indeed, when the old man got up to use the toilet, Alfie almost passed out, believing the old man was about to seise control of the cockpit!

Alfie did not like his uncle. He hardly knew him and found him to be too serious minded. He had only one television and watched soap operas and the news — Alfie couldn't see himself in any of the soaps simply sipping beer in a pub and speaking like a Cockney or a Lancastrian. His uncle had secured Alfie employment on a building site as a general labourer but, despite himself, Alfie couldn't help allowing his imagination running wild. The empty half-built houses were all that was left after a nuclear bomb had exploded. His boiler suit was a special protective overall to guard against the effects of radiation. The cement mixer was not making mortar but was in fact creating a substance that, when ready, would negate the effects of the bomb if applied evenly between the bricks of the buildings. Even the hose took new meaning. When jetting water at full strength, it was a laser that could dissolve people and objects. After a week of this madness, the foreman let Alfie go, and two days later he was back home, much to the relief of his frustrated uncle.

Finally, Alfie got a job and it was perfect. Night security man at a new development. All he had to do was watch programmes on his small portable TV in the security hut and walk around the development once every hour. As Alfie sat in the hut, he imagined he was monitoring the outside world. At the appointed times, he left the hut, put on his hard hat and switched on his torch for his hourly inspection. Only, in the world of Alfie, there was more to it than that. Alfie was guardian of the last trace of civilisation and it was his responsibility to ensure they came to no harm. The hard hat was bulletproof and his torch was a state-of-the-art laser that shot penetrating rays. In short, Alfie was invincible! Stray cats were 'zapped' by his laser, and shadows were attacked with stones as he patrolled the compound. In fact, not only did Alfie enjoy his work – he relished it! The world of Alfie Watters was a safer place, thanks to Alfie Watters.

However, in the post office that morning, Alfie was bored. *Was that old woman all that she seemed? What was taking her so long? And the woman behind the counter – why was she so stern? Was she harbouring a dark secret? What could be in that massive handbag? Had the cashier noticed something that frightened her and made her sit stone faced like that?*

All these things – and more – went through Alfie's mind as he waited.

Mrs Freeman paused in her search and looked closely at the pile of things, she had set on the counter. As well as the biscuit encrusted paper tissues and blood pressure tablets, there were receipts, a number of crumpled envelopes and a dog leash. As she didn't own a dog, the lead confused her which was why she stared so intently at it.

"Mrs Freeman!" Joan said firmly. "You are causing a queue here. I don't wish to hurry you, but have you found your electricity card or do you think that you might find it before closing time?"

Mrs Freeman didn't quite hear every word but she certainly did not like the tone of voice being directed at her by the cashier.

"I have wild trouble with varicose veins, you know!" she retorted. "It kills me to stand as long as this what with the veins and my sciatica and all."

With that, Mrs Freeman began to rummage with renewed vigour through the handbag as Alfie Watters, monitoring the situation closely, wondered if this would be when the gun would be produced.

Suddenly, the serenity of the post office was interrupted by the presence of a masked man who burst into the post office shouting and screaming! In his hand was undeniably a gun of some sort and a plastic bag.

"Everybody down!" he shouted, waving the gun around.

Joan Grace felt faint at the sight of this monster. The eye-holes of the balaclava were uneven, making him look like a gargoyle. Joan froze in terror, her heart pumping faster and faster with each second that passed. Mrs Freeman believed she had heard someone say something behind her and turned as quickly as her arthritic legs would allow her to see what all the commotion was about. Alfie Watters, would-be guardian of mankind, could not believe his eyes! A real gunman! A REAL one too – not just something he imagined! This was actually happening right in front of his disbelieving eyes! It was at that moment, Alfie suddenly realised that he was not a hero. He was beside himself with panic and dropped to his knees as if in prayer for his life.

Mrs Freeman stared blankly at the would-be robber. She didn't notice the gun, which by now was entangled in the plastic bag. She didn't notice Joan Grace duck behind the counter out of sight. All she saw was a strange looking man with one eye peeping through a badly knitted balaclava, and a man praying feverishly nearby. She slowly turned back again and was surprised to see no trace of the cashier, the stern faced one, who she didn't like.

Suddenly, another figure came ambling into the post office, a scruffy, lanky young man with uncontrollable hair and an awkward disposition. He was studying what looked like a giro cheque and seemed oblivious to all that was going on around him. As he walked aimlessly towards the counter still fixated on the cheque, he failed to notice the kneeling Alfie Watters and tripped over his legs. Lurching forward, John Spence waved his arms wildly in a bid to regain his balance. Alfie watched in silent wonder as Spence grabbed the forward-facing robber by the collar of his coat, in a last-ditch attempt to prevent himself from falling. This caused the robber to jerk backwards and lose balance himself. The shiny, we polished floor proved the undoing of John and the robber, as they slipped and slid and collided violently with each other. The first to fall was the robber, straight back on the hard marble effect floor, his head striking the unforgiving surface with force. Lying dazed, he was then attacked by John Spence's bony knee, which crashed into his face as John finally lost all sense of balance and collapsed on top of the robber. Joan Grace heard the yells and smacks and quickly dialled for the police to come, and screamed for her colleague to come out and assist.

"Here it is!" shouted Mrs Freeman in triumph, holding up the elusive electricity card for all to see.

John Spence had no idea what had just happened. Picking himself up, he realised that the giro was missing! The robber managed to raise himself up on one elbow but was too dazed to do anything more than that. It was then that John saw the corner of his giro poking out from below the robber so he shot forward his hand to retrieve it, just as the robber turned around. John's hand seemed to collide with the robber's face in slow motion and the whole building seemed to reverberate at the sound of the robber as John's finger went into the former's visible eye, temporarily blinding him.

"Sorry mate," gasped John as he snatched his giro, relieved to find that it had not been torn.

The noise of sirens drowned out everything else, as the room became illuminated by blue lights flashing through the windows. In no time at all, the police were in the building and had the hapless thief cuffed and lying prostrate on the ground, blinking furiously out of one bloodshot eye. Paramedics spoke soothingly to Joan Grace whose face was devoid of colour. If I survive this day, I will never be back through the doors of this place again, she thought decisively. John Spence sat on a rickety chair trying to establish what had happened, glancing at the clock to see if he would have time to cash the giro before half day closing. Just my luck, he thought remorsefully.

"Could I have your name please, sir?" the officer asked Alfie.

This was it as far as Alfie was concerned. This was to be his moment of glory. He gave his name and then allowed his imagination to run wild.

"I was standing here in the queue, so I was, and that fella came in with a hood on and a gun. He pointed it at me first as obviously I was the greatest risk to him and told me if I did not get down on my knees, he would put one in my head. I got down like he said planning to tackle him from a kneeling position, first chance I got! But, before I knew it, that skinny cove over there came in and attacked the robber. He grabbed him by the back of the neck and pulled him down. The robber crashed to the ground banging his head on the floor, so he did. Next thing I know, Skinny knee'd him in the face, near enough knocking him out! Then, the robber tried to get up and Skinny stuck his finger in the robber's eye, blinding him! I never saw the like of it in my life! The robber never had a chance! That boy might not look like much but he had the robber sorted in about two minutes flat. I am just sorry I didn't get in first but there you go…"

The officer looked at Alfie, then John and finally the robber. It all seemed very unlikely. The skinny chap was sitting staring blankly ahead looking in need of a good sleep. Having made his notes from Witness A: Mr Alfred Watters, the officer strode over to Joan Grace.

"Excuse me, ma'am but could you describe what happened here?"

Joan smiled weakly at the officer and apologised, explaining that as soon as the robber had been distracted by the plastic bag entangling itself with the gun, she had ducked behind the counter until all of the commotion had stopped. All she could confirm was that when she emerged from behind the counter, the robber was lying semi-conscious on the ground with the thin hairy chap kneeling beside him clutching a piece of paper in his hand. The officer nodded silently and looked at Mrs Freeman who was now seated on a stiff wooden chair.

"What can you tell us about the attempted robbery, ma'am?" he asked.

"Robert?" Mrs Freeman bellowed. "I don't know any Robert but I know this! My electric will have run out by now and everything in my freezer will be defrosted!"

The officer raised his eyebrows and studied John.

"Can you tell us what happened here, sir?" he asked the sleepy looking thin man.

"I...well...I don't know, like. It all happened so quickly, so it did. More or less what he said," John replied pointing to an excited Alfie Watters who was speaking rapidly to a paramedic and gesticulating wildly as he spoke.

Madge looked at her son in disbelief, after the police officers had left their home. Admittedly, she had feared the worst when she saw the panda car pull up outside the house. *What carry-on has he been at now?* She had wondered angrily.

As the police officer related the account of the failed robbery, Madge sat blinking in silence. Ronnie sat on the arm of the sofa, his eyes fixed in wonder at his son. *John Spence, their son, had foiled a robbery. John, who counted it an achievement to get out of bed before noon, had saved the day!* John, who was content to sit without moving a muscle for hours each day, had sprang into action and brought a robber to justice.

Her son, John. Not another John Spence, but her son. John.

"Can I have a cup of tea, ma?" John asked sheepishly.

Madge nodded and poured a fresh cup into a waiting mug. There was something not quite right about all this.

"So, run it all by me again, now that policeman has gone," she said slowly.

"Ma, it's really stressful to talk about it," John moaned lazily. "I can't remember all the details of it. I am likely in shock! Anyway, it will all be in the papers because there were reporters there before we left. I didn't get speaking to them as I was in shock but one of the other customers told them all about it. What was his name? Let me think…Oh, aye, that's right. His name was Alfred Watters."

Madge had risen from her well-worn seat to boil the kettle but stopped abruptly. *Hold on a minute*, she thought suspiciously. *I know that name! Oh, my goodness! Alfred Watters! Wee Alfie Watters from Denmark Street! A crazy kid with the wildest imagination known to mankind! I remember him! Running around the supermarket aisles, 'shooting' customers with a bunch of leeks! Told everyone his da was an astronaut because he had got a job as a security man at Belfast airport! Went to England for a week to work and told Mrs Benson he had been away on a mission, to the Far East on behalf of Her Majesty's Government!*

"Was he the only witness?" Madge asked, eyebrows raised.

"Aye, well, he was the only one who saw the whole thing …" John replied sleepily.

Alfie Watters! The maddest fantasist that ever walked! Madge sat down heavily. Then she did something she hadn't done in years. She started to quiver, then shake and then guffawed and brayed loudly. She slapped the table with her hand and shrieked with uncontrolled, hysterical laughter!

John and Ronnie looked at Madge with sheer amazement.

"My son, John!" she bellowed. "A hero!"

The Rookie

Madge Spence sat sullenly at the kitchen table, with a mug of tea in one hand and a ridiculously long cigarette in the other. The Morning Presenters on the TV in the corner were smiling as they spoke, irritating Madge. *How can folk smile and talk at the same time? It's not natural!* Then again, Madge found it increasingly difficult to smile at all. *What is there to smile about in my life*, she wondered glumly. Madge took a long drag of her cigarette and held the smoke in her mouth for an exceptionally long time before exhaling it, slowly, through her nostrils. *A witless husband and a lazy son. That's my lot in life! Speaking of which, where has that idle waster gone? For once in his life, he was awake before 9am and away he went, down the stairs and out the front door without so much as a Good morning, Ma! Idiot*, she thought angrily. *He's likely sleep walking.*

"Any tea in the pot?" her husband asked as he came in from the back yard.

"What? Did the pigeons not make you a cup?" Madge retorted.

Ronnie Spence shot his wife a look of distaste. *She's jealous of the pigeons*, he noted. *Always has been because I spend too much time with them. Well, maybe if she was more civil, I would spend more time with* her. Ronnie poured a measure of weak tea into a cup from the draining board.

"Our John in bed?" he asked, not really interested in what the answer would be.

"Nope, he took off this morning to who-knows-where. Before nine too! He's likely in trouble!"

For the next half hour, Madge and Ronnie sat at the same table, sipping their tea silently. Madge stared blankly at the television screen as Ronnie peered out of the window at his pigeons.

"Has he got a job maybe?" Ronnie ventured, still staring out the window.

Madge looked at him in amazement. *He really doesn't know our John! Imagine even asking that! It's as if he doesn't even live in this house*

"Are you for real?" she bellowed. "Our John *has* a job! It's a day's work getting him out of bed and he manages it at some point every day. That *is* a day's work for that cretin! Now as far as actually leaving home and working for pay, you can forget that! I sometimes wonder if them pigeons have given you bird flu or something, because you're obviously delirious coming out with something like that! *Has he got a job maybe?* He gets tired when folk tell him about *their* jobs!"

She stopped abruptly as if exhausted at her outburst, before heaving her huge frame out of the chair to fetch more milk for another mug of tea. *How did all this happen?* She wondered. *There were no signs of her life turning out this way when we were married. John was a bright baby and could walk and talk before his first birthday. In fact, he walked and talked more than he does now. What a life!*

Ronnie watched his wife lumbering towards the fridge. *How did that happen?* He wondered. *He had married a slim, happy, fun-loving, young woman. She loved him and showed it, and worked hard inside and outside the home. They loved their son, who was bright beyond his years and then, at some point, when he wasn't looking, it all changed. Madge became dangerously heavy and angry with no interest in anything inside or outside the house. John was a disaster. Lazy, weak willed and disinterested in everything. What a family!*

Just then, the front door opened and slammed hard. *Couldn't be John*, they thought. *He wouldn't have the energy to shut a door as hard as that.* They both looked expectantly at the closed door leading to the front hall.

"Well, folks, how are you both?" John asked breezily as he entered the room. "Are you both having a good morning?"

"Are you OK, Son?" Ronnie asked with genuine concern.

"Are you on drugs?" Madge demanded devoid of concern. "Because if you are, you can pack your stuff and get out of here!"

John fell into the armchair nearest the fire and smiled happily at his parents.

"I am certainly OK, Da! And, for your information, Ma, I am not on drugs. I am merely high on life!"

Madge and Ronnie looked at each either with growing concern. It was the first time in years they had actually made meaningful eye contact. They were surprised at the look of terror in each other's eyes and made mental notes to leave it for a few more years, before they would do that again. They quickly looked back to their son, who still wore that silly grin.

"Explain yourself then!" Madge demanded.

"I have got a job!" John replied firmly. "I am soon to be a working man!"

Again, his parents looked at each other despite their rash decision not to do so again for years. *A job???* Their John had just said he had got himself a job.

"Doing what?" Madge asked nervously, unconvinced that John hadn't been to visit a drug dealer.

"I am going to be a policeman." John replied with a pride and confidence that shocked Ronnie and Madge in equal measure.

"You are joking, aren't you?" Madge spluttered.

"Nope!" John said stretching his limbs. "I sat the test and all and I am for training on Friday. In no time at all I will be patrolling the streets of Northern Ireland and keeping the people safe."

Ronnie was dumbstruck as he looked at his son. How had he managed this? Then he noticed that John looked clean and tidy somehow. His hair had been combed and his clothes were sitting right. His shoes looked cleaner than usual and he was wearing a sweater that fitted. Maybe their John actually had gone and got himself a job. But in the *police?* Ronnie had great difficulty imagining him following up on leads and bringing villains to book. And as for clocking in on time or pulling a night shift without sleeping? Forget about it!

"It seems that my actions in the post office last year, where I, single-handedly foiled a robbery, did not go unnoticed. I sat the exam and said nothing because if I had failed it, you would have rhymed on about it for years." He said, nodding at his mother.

Madge stared blankly at her son. *Had he really foiled a robbery?* Oh yes, that's what they all said but who were the witnesses? An old woman who was deaf as a post and hadn't actually seen anything, Alfie Watters a notorious liar and fantasist, and a concussed robber who can't remember a thing about it? Even John hadn't satisfied her with his account of it all which was a word for word reiteration of what that idiot Alfie Watters had said.

"Are you sure about this, son?" Ronnie asked. "I am all in favour of you getting a job, but I'm just not sure this is right for you."

"Oh for goodness sake, Ronnie; Stop pussyfooting around everything! It's our John we're talking about here, not Charles Bronson! Of course this isn't the job for him – though who knows what IS the job for him – but what are you going to do? They all think he's The Equaliser after that carry on in the post office. Even *he* believes it now! Give me strength!"

None of this phased John in the least. He was well aware of the low opinion his mother had of him. His father seemed to have no opinions on anything aside from a fleeting interest here and there. He loved pigeons, because they were undemanding and could not ridicule him. Humans weren't like that so he spent his time with birds as opposed to people. John understood all of this and he also understood his mother. She was unhappy yet had become happy being unhappy. She thrived on misery and the more she focussed on her own mundane life, the more she could fantasise about how it could have been. Aye, Madge loved to hate and thrived on misery. In fact, these were the only things that made her happy.

"Well, like it or not, I will soon be a peeler and that's all there is to it. Criminals beware, don't steal or fence or you'll have to answer to Constable Spence!"

Ronnie stared silently at his son stunned at this poetic outburst. Not since his early years at primary school had John even attempted a rhyme yet here, he was today reciting one he had composed himself. Ronnie was truly amazed.

Madge responded differently by placing her large head in her hands and emitting a very audible groan.

Her John was about to become a peeler! What a job!

When John set off to police training, Madge was at a loss. She had no one to argue with or pick on. It's pointless trying to argue with that docile idiot Ronnie, she decided. He just slinks off out to the back yard to have a gossip with his pigeons. *Dear only knows how John is getting on*, she thought sipping her tea. *I hope they have slip on shoes because I don't think he knows how to tie laces. And that hair! What on earth will they do with that wilderness? They will have to get a hat specially made to go over it.* She giggled mischievously at the thought of it.

The sun streamed in through the cheap living room blinds, and Madge decided that rather than sit inside drinking tea, she would take the bold step of sitting outside on the pavement and get a bit of colour. She pulled the long-suffering chair out and waddled back in to fetch her tea and cigarettes. Exhausted, she sat down heavily on the chair that groaned beneath her.

"Hello, Madge!" a voice screamed shrilly at her. "Isn't it a lovely day? We don't see much of you these days."

That's all I need, Madge thought gloomily. Indigo Barr had a voice that was so high pitched the dogs on the street ran to get away from it. Madge looked up to check that the glass of the street light hadn't shattered.

"A lovely day, Indigo," Madge agreed. "I thought I would get a bit of sun the day. I don't know about seeing much of me, mind you, for there's a right lot of me to see."

Indigo Barr held her hand to her mouth in mock horror at Madge's depreciation of herself.

"Oh, you're a wild woman, Madge!" Indigo screamed back. "I was just wondering how your John is getting on. Is it true he has joined the peelers?"

"He's doing the best," Madge said unconvincingly. "His training finishes in a couple of days so he will be home a day or two and then sent to wherever he will be based."

"Aw that's great!" Indigo smiled. "I must go on here but look after yourself."

Away to spread gossip no doubt, Madge thought. I'm sure she's not one bit interested in my John. The strange thing about Madge was that although she continually railed on John and was forever exasperated at him, she was very protective of him when talking to outsiders.

"Well if it isn't Madge Spence! It's lovely to see you outside the house!"

Madge groaned audibly. Maud Watters was easily the most annoying woman in the whole of Belfast. She and her oddball son were two of the strangest folk Madge had ever met.

"Oh well, why deny the good folk of the city a look at me on a good day?" Madge replied breezily.

"I heard that your John is away off to the police and I think that's great! I never miss Kojak so I know how hard a job it is. Mind you, that Kojak gets through a lot of work in an hour."

Madge could hardly believe her ears. Even for Maud Watters this was bizarre!

"Aye, but sure he has that Stavross to help him," Madge replied sarcastically.

"Oh, I don't think he does a big lot, Madge. Mind you, his hair is a bit like your John's. You know our boys were so lucky to survive the siege of the post office! And your John! Sure, he was the hero of the day! Any wonder he got into the police so easily. My poor Alfie had less luck when he tried to join the army, but he's happy enough doing his wee security job. Nobody will get past him!"

Nobody will get past him because from what I hear all he does is sleep in a hut, thought Madge.

"Well, we will see how it goes," Madge conceded. "He might not be Kojak but he could be Dixon of Dock Green."

"Oh, his shoes were always very shiny! Even in a black and white TV," Maud exclaimed loudly, much to Madge's deepening despair.

"I was speaking to Indigo Barr a wee minute ago," said Madge. "If you hurry, you might catch up with her before she gets her bus."

"Oh thanks, Madge!" Maud gushed, starting to run clumsily down the street. "Give my best to your John!"

Madge shook her head in exasperation as she watched Maud run frantically down the street to catch up with Indigo Barr. *What a pair of gossips together*, she thought. *They'll be talking in short hand to each other to get everything said.* Then, looking at the bright blue sky, Madge shook her head again. *What's the point in me sitting out here? Sure, I don't get a minute's peace.* And with that, she grabbed her seat and mug and headed back inside the house.

The two days John stayed at home after the conclusion of his training flew past. Madge was totally dumbfounded at the change in her son. He was bright, chatty and seemed aware of what was going on out around him. Ronnie even broke away from his precious time with the pigeons to observe his new-found son. In fact, John uttered comments so profound that Ronnie's eyebrows shot up so suddenly and high that it looked like he had grown a fringe. Could it be that John has *matured*, they wondered. *Is the old hapless John Spence gone or is he just taking a rest? Time will tell*, they reasoned. *Time will tell.*

Good fortune seemed to follow John Spence. Everything about him suggested his life would be an unmitigated disaster yet somehow, often at the eleventh hour, good fortune smiles on him. And so it was when John was posted to a local police station meaning, he could live at home and not have to pay for expensive digs somewhere. This suited John well as it would also mean Madge would continue to assume responsibility for his meals and laundry. He would obviously need to give her a few pounds each month, but he figured that he would be earning enough to part with a few twenties to his mother.

On his first day as a real life policeman, John set off proudly to his place of work. He could have worn civilian clothes to the station, but John wanted everyone to know that he was someone now. Not Madge and Ronnie Spence's layabout son, who would never amount to anything but a policeman! As he strode purposefully to the station, folk he knew called out to him and he waved solemnly back. He noticed Alfie Watters coming home from his night shift.

"All the best John!" he yelled. "Shoot a few villains for me today. I will watch the news later to see if you're on it!"

The first few days of full-time employment as a qualified policeman was something of an anti-climax for John. There were no high-speed chases, arrests or newsworthy incidents of any kind. By the Wednesday evening, John's enthusiasm began to wane. As he was leaving, however, the sergeant had good news for him.

"Spence, tomorrow you are going out on street patrol with PC Carter. Be here at 7.45am and report to the front desk."

John welcomed this piece of news. He had been bored rigid learning about procedures, policies and all that kind of thing. Had he not learned all that during his training? Anyway, that's all over now and in the morning, it will be a case of criminals beware! Constable John Spence is on the streets and he takes no prisoners! That night John Spence ate heartily and chatted fluently to his parents. It was all too much for Ronnie who retreated to his pigeons but Madge was engrossed. Her John was behaving in a way that made him seem like a stranger. He was robust and confident, determined to erase crime and be a thorn in the flesh of every lawbreaker in the country. Even though this animated speaker looked like her John, he was totally different. His hair had been trimmed and tamed, his face was smoothly shaven and his eyes were fully open. As she climbed the stairs to bed that night, she felt a little twinge of regret. She missed the old John. The new one gave her no cause for complaint and that left her feeling dejected and as if she had lost her purpose in life. *Let's just hope Robocop down there doesn't mess it all up*, she mused as she went to sleep.

"Good morning!" John shouted cheerily as he entered the police station, scaring the desk sergeant who was drowsily finishing a night shift.

"Is it really, Spence?" the sergeant replied sourly. "I take it this flood of enthusiasm comes from knowing you will be out on the streets today making everyone safe? Well, thank goodness I will be tucked up in bed! At least I will sleep all the safer knowing you are out there."

If John noticed the sarcasm, he didn't let on. He just smiled and nodded happily and strode along the corridor to meet up with Carter. *If he's Carter, I could be Regan,* John mused, comparing them to The Sweeney. When he saw Carter, he dismissed that thought. Carter was a year from retirement and had no plans to make his last year a time of excitement. He had a comic book potbelly with a shock of snow-white hair that made John look comparatively bald. He looked at John through two huge white eyebrows.

"Spence?" he asked gruffly. John nodded and stretched out his hand which was ignored by the older man. "Here's how it is, Spence. I am nearly out of here, time served. I don't want any medals or big headlines for anything. I know you're a bit of a daredevil, and I heard all about how you weighed in at that post office robbery and all. Well, when you're out on the streets with me, forget all that. We will just get our day in with as little fuss as possible, OK?"

John felt somewhat deflated at his companion's attitude, but he reasoned that he would just play along with the old man. There's no point making an enemy of this old warmer, John decided.

As John and Carter prepared to leave the police station, someone else was making preparations for something quite different not too far away. Robbie Coyle had decided when he was young that he wouldn't work for a living. Having seen all of the 'Godfather' movies and 'Good fellas' as well, he purposed to live outside the law and become ridiculously rich. The problem with Robbie was that he hadn't been blessed with any significant measure of wit.

Robbie's criminal career began humbly when he was caught stealing chocolate bars from a newspaper shop. He received a caution from the police and a few sturdy smacks to the ear from his irate mother. He then progressed to shoplifting clothes and adapted a technique, whereby he would take two of everything into changing rooms, slip one set of clothes beneath his own and then casually walk back out from the changing room, with a set intact explaining that they didn't fit. He managed to do this four times before making the mistake of hanging about the shop too long, with the label from the stolen top dangling down from below his own sweater, which in turn was spotted by a shop assistant who alerted security. On that occasion he received a probationary sentence from the judge and his father's belt from his frustrated mother.

Robbie took early retirement from his criminal pursuits after that experience and lived contentedly off his Job Seeker's Allowance benefits (not that he actually sought a job!) and spent his days watching television and dreaming about great riches without the inconvenience of working. One day he watched a programme about the American Mafia and the illegal industry they created 'chopping' cars. It struck Robbie that it would be much easier to get off with stealing a parked car with no witnesses than chocolate or clothes in busy shops where getting caught was almost inevitable – in the case of Robbie anyway. Once, he had the car, he would take it apart and sell the parts to customers, unwilling to pay the full price to legitimate breakers. It never dawned on Robbie that he didn't have the tools to take a car apart. He never thought about where he was going to base his chopping business. In fact, as was typical of him, Robbie saw nothing but the prospect of great riches. He knew how to begin (by stealing the car) and how it would end (by selling off the parts) but he gave no consideration at all about the middle part (finding a place to take his car, strip it down and arrange the parts) never mind finding customers.

And so, it was that as Constables Spence and Carter stepped out onto the streets of Belfast to patrol their designated area, Robbie Coyle was patrolling a car park near the city centre in search of a car. He had no idea how to steal a car even though he had watched thieves, hot wire a range of vehicles on TV. It was all too much for him, all those wires and stinging sparks that sprang from them. So, he contented himself with mooching about, looking through the door windows in the hope that someone had left their keys in the ignition.

It was a bright sunny day, and John talked endlessly about nothing of substance and Carter ignored him completely. He chatters more than the birds, Carter thought to myself, 'This is the first time in my life I wish I was deaf, or hard of hearing at least. He waves at *everyone* whether he knows them or not. This is going to be a long day!'

Meanwhile, Robbie had progressed from looking through windows to trying door handles. As he moved slowly around the rows of cars, he was undecided which one would bring him the greatest profit. Then, just as he was about to give up, he noticed something that made him smile broadly. A Ford Fiesta sat locked but Robbie could see the spare key sitting in the ashtray. Pulling his sleeve down over his hand he made a fist and broke the driver's door window. Robbie let out a scream of pain and danced around for a minute or two, holding the injured hand. He was sure he had broken a couple of fingers as well as the glass. He then reached in with his good hand and opened the door and got inside. His stomach was turning with fear and excitement as he stared at the key, still rubbing his throbbing hand. He had done it! *Riches await me*, he thought triumphantly. *Once I have this car parked up and stripped down, I will be well on my way.* He checked himself out in the rear-view mirror and decided success was looking back at him.

"I am nipping into the shop here to say hello," Carter announced, pointing to the small newsagents across the street. "Do you want me to get you anything?"

"I could take a drink of something, I suppose," John said thoughtfully as if this was a monumental decision.

"OK, I can get you that but wait here. Don't wander off and don't do anything at all until I'm back."

He's like a teacher, John thought resentfully. *He's like a child*, Carter thought angrily.

Robbie was delighted to find that the Fiesta started first turn of the key. He slowly moved off with the remains of his driver door window fully down to disguise the damage he had done. It was a nice day so he was happy to turn up the music and stick his elbow out the window and enjoy the drive.

June McAfee was not happy. She had spent a restless night with a niggling toothache that drove her to distraction. She spent most of the night sipping hot tea and sucking ice cubes in the forlorn hope that one of the two extremes would miraculously kill the pain. When she set off to work she was tired and irritable, determined that a dentist would see her before lunchtime in a bid to end one part of her misery. She parked up and strode angrily to her office block, forgetting to pay the parking fee. She remembered as she got on the lift but reasoned that she would soon be back in the car on her way to a dentist so it didn't matter. After thirty minutes of frantic calls and cancelling appointments, June left her work and jogged to the car.

When she got to the car park, she couldn't believe what she was seeing – or not seeing. Her Fiesta car was gone! She went over to where she had parked it, and there was nothing but a space and a puddle of broken glass. For a moment June forgot about her toothache and stared blankly at the glass. Her car had been stolen! Then the numbness she felt was suddenly replaced by rage. How dare someone steal my car! As she headed purposefully towards the nearby telephone box, the pain returned with a vengeance. Through clenched teeth, June McAfee reported the theft of her Ford Fiesta to the police.

What is keeping him? John wondered, bored rigid. Why should I hang about here all day waiting on him? It really is a beautiful day, so I will maybe take a wee dander down the street.

So, off he went looking over short fences and admiring the neat gardens and colourful hedges. He vaguely heard his radio crackle and a hoarse voice report the theft of a Ford Fiesta car, but he was too busy trying to remember the name of a particular flower to pay much notice.

At that point, Robbie Coyle changed gear as he turned onto the pedestrian street. Pushing the gear stick caused a sharp pain to shoot from his wrist to his elbow. Robbie yelped in response and stared at his hand in shock.

At the same time, John had failed to notice the particularly vicious Jack Russell who took exception to the man in the hat leaning over the fence into his garden. The garden was his domain; his kingdom. Without a moment's hesitation, the Jack Russell charged down the path to dislodge the invader. John spotted the tiny terror just in time and pulled back but still the demonic dog kept coming. John realised if he didn't move quickly, his thin sock would be no defence against those sharp teeth he could see clearly. He spun around and made a break to cross the street, oblivious to the approaching Ford Fiesta car.

At that moment, Robbie glanced up from his aching wrist and was horrified to see a policeman running across the road in front of him. For a split second, Robbie and John locked eyes, both set in terror. John raised his hands in a futile gesture and Robbie slammed his foot on the brake.

Bang! The last thing Robbie saw was the policeman's face pressed against the glass of the windscreen. The last thing John saw was the terrified face of the driver in the Fiesta. The next thing he knew he was on the road, his head on the pavement with a coat below it, looking up to a sea of inquiring faces. After blinking repeatedly in a bid to regain his vision, he focussed on the shocked face of Carter.

"What on earth were you playing at, Spence?" he asked genuinely worried. "When I heard about how you foiled that post office robbery and then seen the cut of you, I admit I didn't believe it. But throwing yourself in front of a stolen car? You have hidden depths, son!"

"I saw the whole thing!" a young woman yelled. "That car came flying down the road swerving all over the place, and this chap ran out in front of it and raised his arms to stop it, and the next thing I knew, he was on the bonnet and then on the road."

"That's right!" said the Council worker in his luminous coat. "He went straight out there and the wee scumbag run him down. I never saw the like of it! I hope you get a medal son. We are sick to the teeth of car thieves!"

Soon, he was back in the back of an ambulance nursing a sore arm, leg and back. He was kept in hospital overnight but released the next morning, his arm in a cast. Ronnie went to collect him but Madge stayed at home to prepare a tea for her injured boy.

As he sat in his favourite chair sipping tea, he related the whole incident to his parents. He had absolutely no recollection of what had happened so he had only the witnesses' accounts to go on. In the absence of any other witnesses, John was content to tell that version of what happened. Ronnie and Madge exchanged looks frequently during the narrative offered by their John. Could it be that he really is a hero of some kind, they wondered. Has he something courageous deep within him that only comes to the surface once in a blue moon?

A knock at the door brought in the local chief superintendent and PC Carter. They fussed and enthused around John who soaked up their praise and admiration as his parents sat dumbstruck. Whilst this was going on, another knock at the door heralded a very grateful June McAfee who presented John with a box of chocolates and a meaningful kiss on the cheek.

"We are extremely grateful to you, Spence," the chief superintendent announced. "What you did was reckless but effective. The driver of the car is now in custody. He claimed he didn't see you until the last second and that he is very sorry he knocked you down. Strangely, he said all he wanted to do was be rich like Roy De Meo. How he planned to do that by stealing a Fiesta is beyond me."

"I will likely be off on the sick break for a while," John said pitifully. "What with my arm like this and my sore back."

"Of course," said the chief superintendent. "Take all the time you need." John smiled.

When they all left, Madge started at her son. *This is all wrong,* she thought. *There's no way her John would run out in front of a car! He could barely run a bath! He'll be lying about now for months on full pay. That hair will be like a bush again before long and he will have bed sores within a month.*

Oh well, she thought, clearing the plates away, *that's what you get when you have a hero for a son. My John! A hero once again.*

She chuckled as she shuffled towards the kitchen. And then, she laughed out loud.

The Wake

All day long, the wind had blown a storm. There wasn't a nook or cranny that the icy blast didn't cut through. Trees long bereft of leaves struggled and strained against the bitter gales. There were no birds on the branches, no blue in the sky and no heat beyond two feet of an open fire.

"I doubt there's going to be a big fall of snow," the granny, forever the weather forecaster, announced to no one in particular but everyone generally. They always wondered how she knew things like that. For as far back as anyone could remember, she had been able to predict the weather with uncanny accuracy.

As they huddled on a thick mat in front of a blazing peat fire, they speculated with excitement about the prospect of a snowfall. It was all the better that the granny had predicted a 'big' fall of snow – the possibilities were endless! Snowballs would be thrown the size of turnips and snowmen would be built the height of the house! Even better, they would build a snow *house*! There would be that much of the stuff, they believed our creations would be there until Easter.

It was Stevie's turn to bring in a fresh bucket of peats, so togged out in wellington boots and a warm coat he bent forward as a challenge to the wind, and stomped off to the peat house, a wooden shed three quarters filled with hard rectangles of turf. As he filled the bucket, he paused to listen to the wind whistling through the gaps in the boards on the sides of the shed. The whistling added to the feeling of the cold air and he quickly returned to the task in hand to get out of the tempestuous winds. It was then that he heard the hard, clattering noise on the tin roof of the shed behind him. As he filled the bucket, the noise grew louder and he stopped to see the cause of the narration. To his shock, the ground outside was white. Snow? Was the granny that quick? Closer examination suggested the dreaded hail. Sure enough, the rattle of hailstones on the tin roof grew louder and the ground was soon completely covered by them. Stevie dreaded the walk back to the house and the effect the hailstones would have on his ears and face. Sure enough, as he ran with the wind at his back and the hailstones attacking all of his exposed skin, he inadvertently squealed with a mixture of pain and excitement.

That night, as he lay in bed, Stevie listened to the wind through the trees and the hail tapping on the window. It was the kind of sound you stopped hearing after a while and as he drifted off to sleep, he wondered if it would turn to snow...

Stevie was awakened by a louder than usual tapping on the windowpane. That hail has got rough, he thought, hoping it was in fact hail, and that the windows would prove strong enough to withstand its relentless attack. Then, it got even louder and he was scared. He thought he heard voices as well but wasn't sure as it might well have been the wind. Then it was unmistakable – someone was banging on the glass and shouting! Terrified, he ran to his parent's room and told them. His father went to have a look, and was confronted through the glass with a windswept cousin. Stevie was sent back to bed and he heard doors opening and closing, followed by muffled voices coming from the kitchen. He got up and pretended to need the bathroom in a bid to hear what was being said. He met his granny and asked her what was going on and she looked steadily at him for a moment before saying quietly, "Your uncle Joe is dead."

Stevie wasn't sure what shocked him most; whether someone had died or the fact that he had an 'uncle Joe'. As he lay in bed after being told the shocking news, he tried to picture this mysterious figure. He definitely had no uncles on his mother's side called Joe, and ran through the names of his dad's brothers and brothers-in-law but drew a blank. He went to sleep believing someone related to us had definitely died but having no idea who it was.

In the morning, it was all explained to the children. The man who had passed away was not actually their uncle but was a brother of their grandfather, making him a great-uncle. Stevie tried desperately to visualise him but to no effect. He had heard folk speak of him and thought he could see an image of an old man sitting by a range saying something, but that was it. He then felt guilty that he couldn't recall him. Stevie looked quizzically at my granny.

"I am sorry uncle Joe is dead," he stammered as if he knew who he was and to let granny know he accepted him as an uncle, even in death.

"Do you remember him, Son?" she asked to Stevie's horror.

"Aye I remember him sitting at a range," he replied, offering my one vague memory in the hope it would satisfy the old woman.

"I think your da is going to the wake the night," she said, looking at him thoughtfully. "Maybe you should go too since you remember him. There won't be many at it in this weather and at his age..."

Now, Stevie had no real reservations about going to the wake with Bill, his father but that was mainly because he had no idea what a wake was. A wake. It didn't sound like anything so there were no clues in the name of it. He spent the rest of the day letting on to know what it was, whilst all the while trying to find out something about it. At teatime, Stevie was instructed to put on his Sunday clothes and then he knew – it was going to be in a church! It was a service for someone who had just died, like a prequel to a funeral.

As they set off through the hail and sleet, Stevie ventured to ask questions that would help him know how to behave. What time did the wake start? Will the minister be there? Would there be a collection? His father sniggered and said it had already started, the minister might indeed be there and there would be no collection. When they drove past the church, he was totally flummoxed and said nothing more for the rest of the journey.

In no time at all, they pulled up at Joe's house. There were several cars parked along the roadside and a few more in the driveway. Although, the lights seemed to be on in every room, the blinds were drawn. Stevie stepped out of the car and into a house of people, some of whom he vaguely recognised and others he didn't know at all. They were all wearing their good clothes, the men in suits and the women in sombre dresses. Although Stevie was something of a stranger, they all seemed to know Bill and spoke to him with familiarity.

In a bid to make himself invisible, Stevie sat on a stool by the window, my back to a piping hot radiator. To his left an elderly man dozed, nursing a cup of tea in his hand. He looked really ancient and snorted occasionally which made Stevie jump but provoked no response from the others apart from the odd sidelong glance. Stevie could smell mothballs and guessed the aroma was coming from the black suit he was wearing which looked as old as the man himself. In front of him, a toothless old lady stared intently.

"Do you not even know your uncle Jim?" she enquired accusingly.

Yet another uncle who, judging by his age, wasn't my uncle at all. Stevie avoided answering by scanning the room and allowing my eyes to alight on an uncomfortable man whom Stevie did recognise. He wore a green suit with a white shirt and a black tie with shiny brown shoes, which looked huge on him. He had his hair swept back tightly and it shone with lacquer. His name was Cyril and he was a notorious bore. He was nodding tight lipped as Stevie's great aunt Eliza spoke about her age and associated ailments. He knew Eliza as she sometimes called at his house with her small husband, Dan and their irritable Pekinese dog.

"It runs in our family, the deafness," she told everyone. "You have no idea what it's like, not knowing what folk are saying!"

"In her case it's maybe just as well," whispered Trevor, a cousin of sorts who always had something to say. Stevie broke into a nervous giggle.

"I'm not completely deaf, you know!" Eliza snapped, wiping the smile from Trevor's face and stopping Stevie giggling mid flow.

"What on earth are they cooking out there?" she wailed. "There's a terrible stink coming from the kitchen. Likely that Joe never cleaned the cooker and that's the cause of it."

"I use a Foreman grill," Cyril offered, nodding solemnly.

"Oh, I loved his films!" Eliza exclaimed. "He was so good on the banjo and could sing so well!"

Cyril looked shocked and then puzzled. Trevor let out a huge sigh of frustration.

"No, FOREMAN," Cyril countered, realising that hard of hearing Eliza was speaking about George Formby.

"If you could see, what I can see, when I'm cleaning windows!" Eliza sang in a shrill voice that made spines tingle throughout the house. Cyril looked desperate to retrieve the conversation.

"Foreman I said, not Formby. He's dead." Cyril explained.

"The boxer?" asked Eliza clearly shocked. "He's dead? Oh my goodness, I never knew that and he was so good in the kitchen. I saw him on the TV with his apron on and all! I never knew he was dead! They say these things come in threes. First poor Joe and now George Foreman!"

Eliza began to effect a series of wails and dabbed her eyes with a handkerchief. Cyril was beside himself and looked around the room wildly as If to convince us all that none of this was his fault.

"Aw what have you done, Cyril?" Trevor asked mischievously, fully aware of what had happened, but seeing an opportunity to make Cyril feel bad. "Has that poor woman not got enough to contend with?"

June, Eliza's daughter then came rushing in from the kitchen.

"What's wrong with my mum?" she asked, her eyes wide.

"Cyril made her cry," Trevor said unhelpfully.

Cyril shook his head vigorously but the hair remained Intact. He nervously rubbed the palms of his hands up and down his trouser legs and seemed dumbstruck. He then paused to glare at Trevor before getting up and leaving the room in a hurry. Suddenly, Uncle Jim, fast asleep since we arrived, sat upright and looked all around the room.

"Well, thank goodness for that! He puts years on me and I have had to sit here pretending to sleep for the last hour waiting for him to go!"

Everyone laughed at Jim's outburst which was interrupted by a loud knock at the door.

"Hello, June, sorry to hear about Joe!" a voice gushed. "I am here on behalf of my mother. She's all out in a rash. Maybe German measles or maybe scarlet fever! Could be anything…she might not even see Christmas!"

No one paid much heed to the newcomer, and his morbid report on his mother's health. Everyone present either knew Alfie Watters personally or by reputation. He was a fantasist who exaggerated everything.

"Or maybe none of the above?" Trevor suggested.

Alfie came in and sat down oblivious to Trevor's obvious insult. He looked around the room studying each person present.

"Did you say your brother is ill?" Eliza asked.

"No, my MOTH-ER," Alfie replied breaking the word into two syllables.

"Oh, my mother is long dead, son, but thanks for asking," Eliza countered.

"The drifts along the next road are twenty feet high if they're an inch!" Alfie announced, unaware that almost everyone there had travelled that same road that evening and knew his report was utter nonsense.

"Has that idiot Cyril been placed by another idiot?" Uncle Jim asked in his usual angry tone. "Dear help this poor country! During the war we were men when we were sixteen but today young ones haven't even an IQ of sixteen!"

Alfie seemed oblivious to the insult directed at him and, encouraged by the mention of the war, began to tell a totally irrelevant story about a soldier. The slight pauses in his discourse served as proof that he was making the whole thing up, and everyone lost interest and began talking amongst themselves. Stevie found the whole thing fascinating and moved away from the angry Uncle Jim and from sight of the toothless lady to sit beside a quiet middle-aged man, who hadn't spoken to anyone. Feeling manly, Stevie decided to initiate a conversation.

"Hello there," he said breezily. "I am Steven, Bill's son."

"My name's Robbie. I am sorry, I don't know, Bill."

"That's him over there," Stevie said pointing to his father. "My da, Bill."

"I am sorry, son but I don't actually know anyone here," said Robbie apologetically. "I just read in the paper that the old man had died and folk told me this is a great house for food, so I thought I would pop in and have some."

Stevie was truly amazed. He might not know much about wakes but he was certain that if you're going to attend one, you should at least KNOW the recently bereaved or a member of the family. Stevie looked at the two neat rows of small, perfectly cut triangular sandwiches, a row on each leg. Robbie smiled contentedly at Stevie.

"Are you serious?" Stevie asked.

"Oh aye, I certainly am. The food is indeed very pleasing and very tasty."

Stevie decided to move away from Robbie. He was in a class of his own when it came to the competition for having a brass neck! Alfie was now reduced to speaking to Cyril who had returned from his exile in the kitchen and seemed content to listen as opposed to speaking. The toothless woman scanned the room intently, whist wiping her mouth with a handkerchief in a bid to mop up the particles of food that escaped as she ate and talk at the same time.

"Now, would you like to go up and see him?" June asked kindly.

"Who?" Steven asked, fearing another unknown 'uncle' awaited him.

"Your uncle Joe of course!" snapped the toothless woman, spraying small pieces of food around Trevor whose eyes widened at the sight of the foodstuff on his sleeve.

Stevie looked to his dad with pleading eyes, silently asking him what he should do. Bill nodded slowly and broke away from uncle Jim, who had begun a tirade against traffic wardens and parking fees. His reasoning was that he had fought in the war, so had paid his dues so he would park where he liked. Toothless nodded in agreement, her eyes scanning the room as if looking for any disagreement.

When Stevie entered the dimly lit bedroom, he saw the gleaming wood of the coffin to one side and a row of occupied seats to the other. Eliza was there already telling everyone that poor Mrs Freeman from the Tuesday Club had been caught up in a robbery when going in to pay her electricity bill at the post office.

"Are you here to see him?" Eliza said, abruptly ending her report of the post office robbery.

Bill nodded, and he and Stevie stepped forward towards the coffin, led by Eliza who stopped parallel with Uncle Joe's head.

"Aw, would you look at him!" she exclaimed. "Sure, doesn't he just look like himself?"

Stevie was confused. Who else would he look like? Bill's eyebrows shot up so high it looked like he had grown a second fringe. Stevie peered into the coffin and there he was; Uncle Joe, serene and quiet, never again to sit at the range. After a slight and somewhat unnerving pause, Eliza ushered them out of the room and down the stairs.

"More tea, anyone?" June asked.

Robbie nodded eagerly, and offered his empty cup. Stevie noticed that the two former rows of sandwiches that had adorned his legs had since been reduced to a few crumbs.

"There's only so much tuna a man can eat," Trevor said and Stevie nodded knowingly. He had restricted himself to biscuits and fancy buns. Wakes were OK, he decided. No TV but plenty of interesting people and good pastry. He smiled at Robbie, as if to indicate that the old man had been right about the food.

Again, a blast of cold air attacked Stevie's legs as the back door opened and closed again. Stevie didn't know the squat woman before him in the headscarf. She wheezed loudly as she fought her way out of a thick overcoat. Her face was almost purple and Stevie noticed huge curls below the scarf which the woman carefully removed and stuffed on her pocket, reaching out and grabbing the doorframe as if to maintain her balance.

"So, what happened to him?" the heavy woman demanded of no one in particular.

"Good old Madge!" Trevor said loudly. "About as subtle as a swinging brick!" Then looking at the woman he said simply, "His pulse and heart stopped and that was it."

Madge Spence glared at Trevor. She had never liked him, but then Madge never seemed to like anyone so Trevor thought nothing of her glare. June produced a narrow wooden kitchen chair that soon disappeared below Madge, who sat down heavily on it.

"Poor Joe!" wailed Eliza. "What could have happened to him?"

Uncle Jim looked at Eliza as if she had split the atom.

"What do you mean what could have happened to him? You're as bad as sour puss Spence over there! He turned 93 on his last birthday, that's what happened him!"

Madge quickly lost interest in the cause of death when another woman offered her a cup of tea and a tray of sandwiches. Madge used her huge hands t envelope the cup and lift at least four of the dainty sandwiches.

"I would say he left a pound or two," she said biting viciously into a sandwich…looking round the room she added, "Though, he didn't leave much of worth in the house, I see."

"What about that man of yours and your son, Madge?" the toothless woman asked malevolently. It was well known – mainly because Madge had made it well known – that Ronnie Spence hadn't worked since the shirt factory closed eight years ago and their son John had never worked a day in his life.

Madge ignored the question and continued to speculate on the estate of the late Joe McConnell.

"I dare say I will get a wee lift," Trevor suggested. "After all, I called in to see him back and forth and fixed his fence this past summer."

"And that should get you a mention in the will?" Eliza asked in a shrill squeal. "Many a time, I hoovered this carpet and made him his tea. I never asked for a thing but I am sure he was good enough to remember me when he made his will."

"I am his only surviving brother, so I expect I will be handling his affairs," Uncle Jim stated with authority.

"Well, Joe and me go back a long time as you all know," said the toothless woman. "I know we never married but we were as good as…and many a time Joe said if it had ever been in his head to get married, it would have been me."

"So, in other words it never entered his head!" Eliza snapped. The speculation about Joe's money had improved her hearing significantly.

Robbie broke the ensuing strained silence, each person in the room lost in thought about how much they might inherit.

"Is there any more tea only this time with some sugar?" he enquired. Everyone looked silently at him and then looked away to return to their thoughts of greater riches.

It was late when Stevie and Bill left the house and returned through the bumpy hail encrusted roads to home.

"Well, what did you think of your first wake?" Bill asked his son, bemused.

Stevie gave the question a great deal of thought. It was certainly a very strange experience, he thought. He hadn't realised that he was related to so many strange characters or that his family had such strange friends like that Madge who had started the row about who was getting what or that Alfie who's lies and exaggerations had been breathtaking. He also wondered about Robbie, the sandwich eating, tea-drinking stranger who felt no shame to having gatecrashed a wake.

Bill kept his eyes on the road as he drove slowly, the hail having given way to sleet.

Stevie also considered the rage of his 'uncle' Jim, and the monotonous Cyril who had caused it. Then there was the fairly normal but worn out June who kept bring tea and sandwiches as well as a few buns out from the kitchen, unnoticed by most but met with excitement by Robbie. Eliza was nice but went on a bit and seemed a bit too fond of misery and suffering for Stevie's liking. It was likely because she was old that she seemed to thrive on these things. He noticed that his granny was an avid fan of the death notices in the local newspaper and would read them aloud to anyone present. If it was someone she knew, she would be almost excited. She also spoke a lot about folk who had died and others who were very ill. Eliza was of similar disposition.

"Who was the toothless woman? Was she my aunt?" Stevie asked sleepily.

"In some ways," replied his father somewhat mysteriously. "She was a very special friend of you Uncle Joe."

Stevie wasn't sure if that made her an aunt or not and as his father seemed reluctant to discuss the matter further, he let it go. He thought about Trevor and decided he was his favourite out of everyone at the wake. He was funny and naughty, willing to annoy folk and get off with it. Stevie hoped that one day he would be able to do that because at present, if he annoyed someone deliberately like that, he would be punished. Yes, Trevor was someone to be admired and, one day, emulated.

"Well?" his father asked. "What did you think of the evening?"

"I think when my time comes, I won't have one," Stevie said drowsily. "I wouldn't want all that madness going on around me, and I not fit to enjoy it."

As he fell asleep, the sleet turned to snow and he heard his father chuckling softly at his response.

Snow...the granny had been right...

The Tent

With the summer holidays fast approaching, everyone seemed preoccupied with making plans for July and August. Simon Stewart listened with ill-concealed envy as his classmates related previous foreign holidays and boasted of their pending fortnight abroad this year again. Spain, France, Greece and even America!

"What about you, Simes?" asked Ian Jackson whose father owned a mill. "Where are you going this year?"

Simon recognised it for what it was; a general question. These people aren't asking where I am going to on holidays to demean me, them being fully aware that I am going nowhere. They are just typical rich kids who assume *everyone* enjoys a sun kissed holiday abroad in summer.

"Not sure yet," Simon replied truthfully as he wasn't sure whether he would spend a day in Portrush or a day in Portballintrae.

"Well, make sure and have a good time wherever you go!" Jackson replied cheerfully.

"Aye, I will do. Enjoy Paris and be sure to leave it as you found it!" Simon replied heroically.

As he walked home from school on that last day of term, Simon was relieved to get a break from the place. Grammar school was not for him at all though, as he was useless with his hands, it was his only option if he wanted a job later in life. He was also glad to be away from his foolish talking middle class peers who irritated him on a daily basis. They meant no harm but they lived in a bubble; a bubble of privilege and getting whatever they wanted. Nothing meant anything to them, he noted many a time. What Simon would work hard for every Saturday for two months, they would be *given* by their over-indulgent but neglectful parents. If they lost it or broke it, it didn't matter as it would be replaced with little effort; and no effort on their part.

Being completely honest, Simon had absolutely no interest in a foreign holiday. All that hassle of packing, getting to the airport then waiting hours and then being herded onto a plane like sheep? Going to stay in a hotel full of strangers with no say who your neighbours will be? And then when you get there, what is there to do? You have to share a pool with loads of folk, and if you go to the beach, you have to virtually fight your way to a patch of sand to lay down your towel. Simon grimaced as he tried to imagine all that and decided it wasn't for him. He imagined going into a café for something to eat, and neither understanding the menu nor the waiter, and leaving the place hungry, after inadvertently ordering something inedible. He shook his head violently at the thought of it. No, he decided firmly, I am far better off at home.

Still, he wondered, what *will* I do for two whole months...

Simon's decision was made for him when he arrived home to find that the farmer, he worked for on a Saturday, would be needing him for the first week in July and most of August. This did not disappoint Simon in the least. Big Jim Shannon was a mountain of a man, who did the work of any three ordinary men half his age. He expected 14-year-old Simon to keep up with him and do two days' work in one at the very least. Yet there were three things about Big Jim Shannon that Simon admired. Firstly, he had a huge appetite and his wife insisted that Simon should eat as much as her workhorse husband. In fact, the food tasted so good that Simon often felt he would work there for the food alone. The second thing was that you never had to ask Big Jim for your wages because as the working day drew to an end, he produced the cash from his pocket and thrust it into your hand with shocking force. The third thing was that Big Jim wasn't afraid to allow Simon to drive tractors, talk politics and ask his opinion on things, he had heard on the news. It comforted Simon to think that the Big Man could learn as much from him as the other way around. Big Jim was a man's man and he treated Simon like a man.

Simon left his home immediately on receiving the message and cycled to the farm to ask when exactly Big Jim would require him. Big Jim wasn't a man who specified times and dates. If Simon asked him the time, his reply would be related to meal times. For example, any time between 9 am and 12 noon, it would be 'Heading for lunchtime', or if it was after 1pm, it would be 'Heading for tea time'. Ask big Jim when Easter would fall this year and he would reply, 'Tail enn o the Spring'. Likewise, Christmas occurred 'Roon or aboot the turn o the year'. So, Simon sought a specific set of dates and times he knew it would be impossible for Big Jim to give him.

Big Jim was in boisterous form when Simon met him, charging across the yard and spent little time telling his young helper to call back 'nearhand the Twelfth' which indicated on or about 12th July. Simon suggested the first day of July and Big Jim, who was already on his way to his next task, shouted back, "Aye that would be OK."

So that was Simon set up for the most of the summer with work, food and cash and expanding muscles as a handy side effect of his toil on the farm.

On his way home, Simon noticed two of his friends sitting on the grass ditch near the road. He stopped with them to ascertain their plans.

"Naw much," offered Rodney Sloan. "It will be a long summer at this rate."

Benny Graham simply shrugged his shoulders as if he had nothing in his mind whatsoever.

"Will we head down to Davy's?" Simon suggested in a bid to save his pals from their summertime blues.

Both sighed in response and got up lazily from the grass. Simon decided to abandon his bicycle, placing it behind a nearby shed. His friends were travelling on foot so it was pointless him doing otherwise. In a few minutes they found themselves at Davy McKee's house and duly knocked the door, waiting in expectation for their friend to appear. When the door opened, it was his mother who indicated that Davy was in the garage. The three friends strolled slowly in the direction of a tin shed, their steps tired and lazy in the summer heat. Pushing the door open, they saw Davy standing with his back to them staring at the ground before him. He made no effort to look around so they walked across to join him, intrigued at what demanded so much concentration. Standing beside their friend, looking where he was looking, didn't help at all.

"What is it?" Rodney asked.

An indescribable tangle of strings, metal rods and something that resembled canvas lay before them. None of them had ever seen the like of it all before so all eyes turned to Davy in their search for enlightenment. That proved to be a pointless exercise as he just stood there silently staring at the jumble.

"Is it *anything*?" Benny asked, his brow furrowed in puzzlement. "Or is it just a pile of different things lumped together?"

After another minute that felt like an hour, Davy whispered in disbelief,

"It's a tent."

None of the boys had ever seen a tent before up close and even then, they had been pitched and looked like a tent. It seemingly never occurred to them that the un-pitched tent would look like this!

"How do you go about making all of this stuff look like a tent?" Rodney asked, still staring at the mess in front of him.

"Never mind *look like* a tent," Simon countered. "How can we make it actually *be* one?"

"I don't honestly know," Davy confessed. "I bought it for a fiver off Jim Porter and he swore that it's a tent and it is right and easy built up into one."

"And where exactly would we build it up into one?" Benny asked with concern. "Sure your ma's garden is full o flowers and the like. There would be no room for that!"

Luckily for the boys, the garage was largely empty except for the tent so they decided to pitch it where it lay. After much grunting and groaning and using language they hoped Mrs McKee would not hear, they had the tent built up. It sagged here and there and it appeared to be inside out but aside from that, it was a tent of sorts.

"Well, at least we know all the bits are there," Simon said with optimism. "So when we go camping, we will have the room and the parts to build it right."

"Are we even going camping?" Benny asked, "For it's the first I heard of it if we are!"

Davy looked at his friend as if Benny was insane.

"Of course, we are going camping! What's the point of having a tent if we don't? Anyway, my da parks his car in here so it will need to be taken down for now."

And so, the boys set about dismantling the tent, taking care to assemble the various parts in ways that would make the pitching of it easy when the time came.

Joe Watters had worked in the garage in the centre of the village for as long as anyone could remember. He would take grossly extended breaks to regale the younger generation with tales of horse drawn carts, threshers and ancient machinery he had fixed as a youth. The older ones didn't seem to believe many of Joe's tales but Simon, Benny, Davy and Rodney made a willing and easily convinced audience who were only too eager to believe every word he said. There were times they wondered if maybe he would exaggerate a little but, aside from that, they were content to accept his genius at face value.

"A tent, you say?" Joe asked the boys when they told him of their newest acquisition, reasoning that when you need advice, who better to go to than the man who knows everything. They nodded enthusiastically.

"Well, you would be best to pitch it in one of your gardens," Joe advised. "That way, if something goes wrong during the night, you won't have far to go to get a bed."

If something goes wrong the boys wondered? What could possibly go wrong? You pitch the tent, put in sleeping bags and sleep. Then the next morning you get up and take the tent down and go home.

"Sure, what could go wrong?" Davy asked, putting everyone's fears into words.

"You never know these days," Joe sighed. "Mind you, there were always bad folk about. Poor old da was working in London and saw Jack the Ripper! Now, he was a bad one, all right. He was a killer!"

The boys sat staring open mouthed at Joe. Could this be true? Was there someone called Jack the Ripper?

"What did he do, this Jack?" Benny asked, his eyes huge.

"He tore them apart with knives!" Joe said almost cheerily. "He wore a black cloak and had a massive black hat and a great big bag of knives! My poor old da never got over it either. On that terrible night my da was walking to his lodgings and a man stopped him for a light for his pipe. My da gave him a light and the man says, 'Thank you very much, sir. My name is Jack. Who are you?' And my da says, 'I'm Fred Watters. Good night to you.' Well, my da says this Jack carried a bag and when he walked off, there was a clattering sound coming from the bag, like knives bashing into each other. And when my da looked back, there was a stain that looked like blood on the pavement where Jack had set the bag to get the light. The next morning my da saw in the papers that a woman had been cut up and killed in the very street where he had seen this Jack. Later that day, it came out that the killer of the woman was called Jack the Ripper! Well, my da knew rightly he had been a witness and he thought that Jack would come after him so he hooked it there and then and came straight home on the boat to Belfast!"

The boys were speechless. There was just too much detail in this story for it to be a lie. They gaped at Joe Watters in the hope he would laugh; that it had all been a joke and they would laugh too. Only, he didn't laugh and neither did they.

"What happened to that Jack?" Rodney ventured to ask.

"No one knows, son," Joe said thoughtfully. "They never ever caught him. He got clean away with it all."

"But that was ages ago so surely he would be dead by now?" Simon asked hopefully.

"Look, forget about Jack," Joe said, as if just remembering that he was employed to do a job. "Stay away from the forth and you'll be fine."

The boys had never considered camping at the forth, an ancient mote and bailey about a mile from the village. It was just a huge mound of earth with trees growing on it and swampy murky water around the base of it. It was a great place to find frog spawn and make swings from the huge tree branches but it wasn't in their view a campsite. Yet they were intrigued by Joe warning them to stay away from it.

"Why should we not camp at the forth?" Davy asked defiantly.

"Well you see, hundreds of years ago this place was crawling with druids. They were rare boys who wore long white dress like things and big hoods. They were wizards and done magic things and cast spells on folk. Anyhow, when they died there was nowhere to bury them so they went to where the forth is now and stood their dead ones up and shovelled earth around them. They believed that their dead ones would wake up so that's why they buried them standing up. After a while, there were loads of them dead so they ended up with a big massive mound of earth but there were no headstones in them days so they planted a tree for every druid buried there. That's why it's a big mound today with loads of big trees on it. Don't be camping there because it's a graveyard of wizards and they might even come back and have you for disturbing them."

The boys walked away from Joe and didn't notice him chuckling at them as they left. They didn't speak until they were on their own.

"Do you all believe what Joe said, about that Jack the Ripper and the druids and all?" Simon asked, pretending to be casually asking a question but really hoping the others would tell him it was all a load of nonsense.

There was a mixed reaction to his question and they parted company unsure of whether Joe Watters had been telling the truth or not.

After supper, Simon decided to consult his parents in a quest to have his fears put to rest.

"Was there such a person as Jack the Ripper?" he asked, his voice sounding high-pitched with worry.

"Oh aye," his father replied immediately. "He was a mad man who lived in London and went out at night killing women."

Simon felt himself weaker; Joe Watters had been telling the truth after all! Jack the Ripper was *real*! Not only did he actually exist but he had killed women at night in London, just as Joe had told them.

"Was he not caught though?" Simon continued, desperately hoping the police had brought this monster to justice.

"Nope," his mother answered. "No one ever knew who he was."

Simon couldn't believe it! For all they knew he could have escaped to Ireland and maybe even lived near them. He would be very old now but still dangerous with his big bag and the knives rattling about inside it. There was just one more detail.

"Did he smoke a pipe?"

"Right you, it's time for bed!" his father said sternly. What had gotten into this young boy? Did Jack the Ripper smoke a pipe?

As he headed to the door, Simon paused. He might as well hear all the bad news and get it over and done with.

"Just one last thing; Was Jack the Ripper a druid or did they not really exist?"

"Get to your bed and put all that nonsense out of your head or you won't sleep tonight! Druids were about a long time before Jack the Ripper!"

That was it then! As he climbed the stairs to bed with the lights on, Simon realised that Jack was real and so were the druids. They might all be dead now but they were all standing under trees at the forth waiting to make a comeback when the time was right. As he drifted off to sleep, he contented himself with the belief that had the druids been in London when Jack was out and about, they would have sorted him out once and for all...

The next day Simon broke the bad news to his friends. They looked at him with a mixture of disbelief and horror as he confirmed the existence of pointy-headed druids and one Jack the Ripper. As they sat in silence evaluating Simon's information, Davy suddenly blurted out:

"I don't care if it's true or a lie! I think we should go camping this weekend! And we should camp at the forth!"

The others looked at him as if he was insane. The *forth*? After everything that had been said? And *this weekend?* It was already Thursday so he really meant the very next night! But that was Davy all right; the more the risk the bigger the thrill! Each of the others hesitated before speaking, wondering who should speak first. Then, one by one, they all unconvincingly agreed. They would camp at the forth that weekend.

"Unless some of you are too scared," Davy added smiling.

This was met with guffaws of scorn from the others, as if the very thought of being afraid was ridiculous beyond words. Laughing loudly was also a great way of hiding the fear they each felt, they found. And so it was agreed so they spent the next hour deciding who would bring what and they parted company to break it to their parents that they would be camping out tomorrow night.

As agreed the day before, they met at Davy's house at 2pm on the Friday. Each had with him the essentials for camping. Benny provided matches, firelighters and two flasks of hot water. Simon had bread, butter, jam and a knife plus an assortment of biscuits and Rodney came armed with a huge battery lamp, two tins of beans and crisps and juice. Davy bore only the tent but it was accepted that given the weight of it, that was more than enough for one chap to carry. They bound their rolled up sleeping bags with twine, slung them over their shoulders and set off down the rough stone lane. They crossed a huge field and remarked about the strong sun and the heat as they stumbled along, forgetting all their fears, their excitement growing with every unsteady step.

After what seemed to the boys like ages, they were confronted with a buzzing single wire that ran the full length of the field. It was an electric fence, placed there by the farmer to partition his field. Cows looked at them with disinterest as they each laid down their burdens and stared at the wire.

"We will be able to go under it," Rodney said confidently. "We will stoop in below it and then drag our stuff through and get going."

"How come every now and then the buzzing gets really loud and then dies away again?" Benny asked with a fascinated look on his face as he stared at the wire.

"The actual charge only comes now and again," Davy replied knowingly. "That way it doesn't use as much electric."

"Would it kill you?" Benny asked worriedly.

"Hardly!" Simon replied loudly. "If it could kill, then it would kill the cows and what use would that be?"

"Prove it!" Davy challenged. "Put your hand on the wire and see what happens."

"I can't be bothered," Simon replied, trying to disguise the fact that he was too frightened. The others then started to dare him to grab the wire.

"OK, if you do it, we will all do it," Davy said, looking at the other two who stopped shouting immediately.

Tentatively, they stepped forward together and lightly touched the wire, withdrawing their hands suddenly before the surge went through their fingers. Looking at each other with alarm, they heard the dull clunk as the electricity passed harmlessly along the wire.

"Now!" Davy shouted. "It will be two minutes before there's another surge! Grab it!"

In unison, they grabbed the wire and closed their eyes tightly, silently counting to 120, unaware that Davy had no idea when the next surge would pass through the electric fence. As they got to 52, the wire sprang to life, the dull clunk signalling the electrical surge. Simultaneously, all four boys screamed in terror as the shock attacked their hands, travelling up to their elbows. It only lasted a few seconds but to the boys it felt like hours. They finally let go of the wire and rolled around the grass in exaggerated agony. After a lot of screaming and writhing, they sat on the grass, rubbing their arms and staring at Davy.

"What?" he asked defensively. "You all counted too slowly!"

Disgruntled and offended at their friend's betrayal of trust, they lifted their stuff and ducked under the raging wire, walking a few steps ahead of Davy who sniggered helplessly.

The cattle the wire had been designed to contain had left their marks intermittently across the field and when Rodney stepped in the evidence in a once-white plimsoll, the others found it hysterically funny. However, by the time they reached the hedge to the field where the forth stood, all four of them had done likewise.

After ten minutes of struggle, the four managed to fight their way through a thorny hedge, albeit taking many of the thorns with them in their clothes.

"I'm all scabbed!" Benny wailed, pulling briars from the sleeve of his jersey. "These scrapes will all fester too. They always do!"

"Worse still," Rodney said wickedly, "they might be poisonous thorns. You could die the night!"

Benny wailed even louder, frantically pulling off his sweater and examining the cuts as he stumbled along.

"There's a wee burn beside the forth," Simon said, seeking to pacify his friend. "You can wash your arms in it and that will get rid of the poison."

In reality, Simon had no idea if washing in a polluted river would help or if his friend had even been poisoned but he reckoned that such advice would settle him down, which it did and the wailing was replaced with a hopeful look.

Finally, the boys reached their destination. This ancient landmark had stood silently for many centuries, quietly surveying the surrounding countryside. The lofty thick trees that grew from the huge mound stared at the boys as they looked in wonder at the sight. Surrounded by a swampy moat of black water and buzzing flies, this was the stuff of films. And here they were, just four local chaps, preparing to become part of the history of the forth. They had been here before, of course, but only for an hour or two and always during daylight. For the first time, they paused long enough to take in the awesome sight of the forth and thought about their sketchy knowledge of the history of it. This was going to be a great night!

"Right boys, sort the tent," Davy commanded, assuming charge as owner of the tent. "Where did Benny go?"

Hearing a splash, they looked over to see him in the burn, bent over and up to his knees in water, his arm below the waterline in a frantic bid to neutralise the effects of the poison. Each of the others shook their heads in disbelief at the naivety of their friend.

In about 10 minutes, the tent was spread out across the uneven surface of the forth. To one side of it lay an assortment of poles and rope with a few bent pegs – *too few*, Simon thought. The boys then set to work trying to make sense of all the bits and pieces. Rodney crawled inside the canvas and stood upright in a bid to find out what it should look like. The others busied themselves with the poles and ropes wondering how it seemed to go together easier in Davy's garage than out in the open. There was much arguing and accusations before the tent stood erect, after a fashion. The group stood back, three of them inspecting the structure before them as Benny inspected his arm for signs of decay.

"Looks like there's something missin'," Rodney announced, stating the obvious as they all stared at the deep hollow in the middle. "Like a pole to run along the top of it maybe?"

"There's no maybe about it!" Davy snapped. "It must have fell out along the way as it was in the garage when we put it up. Likely cutting through thon thorn hedge!"

"It will do all right!" Simon suggested, not wanting to have to trek back to retrieve the pole. "It doesn't look like it will rain so it won't matter."

The boys all nodded in agreement and decided to explore the area, leaving the bedraggled tent standing forlornly amongst the trees. As they walked, they ate some of the food they had brought with them, wondering if it might be a good idea to tie some rope from an overhanging branch to make a swing.

"You can't do that!" Benny shouted in alarm. "It would be sacrilege! OK, we done it before and all but that was away back before we knew what the trees were. You heard what Joe Watters said. The trees are more or less headstones. You can't swing from a headstone! It just wouldn't be right!"

The rest glared at Benny. He was right and they were angry that he was right because it meant they would be denied a swing.

"We could make a hut!" Rodney suggested. "There are plenty of branches and things."

"What's the point of making a hut when we have a tent?" Davy asked, afraid that the desire for a hut would negate the need for his tent.

"I don't know," Rodney replied. "I just thought we could make one. Not for us, like, but for other ones who might come here."

Davy seemed content with that reasoning and they set to work gathering whatever branches and grass they could lay their hands on. At last they had created a hovel of some kind that lacked any grace or sense of style. It would only fit two of them in a crouched position but that was not the point. In fact, nothing was the point as the whole notion of a hut had simply seemed like the right thing to do in the absence of any other ideas.

"Here, it's getting dark!" Rodney exclaimed. "We better get back round to the tent and set a fire."

Davy reached into the 'wall' of the hut and retrieved a bundle of dry sticks and twigs, leaving a gaping hole. The others looked at him accusingly.

"Well, we need these for the fire and the hut needed a window so there you go!"

At the tent, the boys managed to start a modest fire using the sticks and twigs that had once been part of the hut. They had lost all track of time and the sun was setting as the fire ignited. They all sat around the noisy fire looking at the long shadows being cast by the trees and told each other how it would soon be dark but that they weren't a bit scared. It would be a great night and they would do it again before long, they agreed.

Believing it to be very late, but really only 10 o'clock, they decided to stoke up the fire and settle down to sleep. They each looked around themselves, trying to appear nonchalant but secretly feeling a tinge of fear. The tall trees now *looked like* monuments to the dead, tall and silent, foreboding even. The gurgling of the nearby burn sounded sinister in the night as the water moved over the stones in an endless race. Night birds squealed messages to them in a pitch much too high to sound harmless. No one wanted to be the last one in the tent so they fought and pushed their way into it as if the thin canvas would protect them in any eventuality.

"Put the battery lamp on!" Davy ordered. "Just so we can see what we're doing," he added quickly as if to dispel notions that he might be wary if not afraid of the dark.

In a short time, all four boys were below jackets and blankets nibbling at biscuits.

"This is great!" Rodney exclaimed in a bid to convince himself and others that he preferred this to his warm, comfortable bed at home. "I mean, we should do this all the time."

"All the time?" Benny repeated in question form. "I don't know about that but, aye, it's great, right enough!"

"What about that Joe Watters though?" Davy snorted scornfully. "I mean, did you ever hear nonsense like that!"

The others laughed nervously, hoping that Joe had been joking the whole time.

"Aye he's a silly talking man, right enough," Simon offered, "though according to my folks at home there *was* a character called Jack the Ripper."

No one spoke.

"My da said he was a killer too. He used a knife and maybe even a whole bag of them, like Joe said. He went out only at night, when it was pitch black, and he caught folk and cut their throats clean open!"

"Adults or wee children?" Benny asked fearfully.

"Either!" Davy replied, suddenly knowledgeable about the Victorian murderer. "He killed the first ones he seen and he never knew if they were men, women or children because it was that dark, there was no way of knowing!"

Rodney and Benny now thought about their own beds and the safety offered to them by their homes and families. Simon swallowed water in a bid to settle his fluttering stomach.

"Was he worse than the Druids?" Benny asked, the fear evident in his voice.

"Ah now they were bad," Rodney said knowingly. "I heard they killed all round them. They didn't like strangers at all and if they spoke to you in a funny language and you didn't answer them in it, which was it! They killed you on the spot!"

"I don't believe that!" Davy shouted, not wanting to believe it. "I heard they were all peaceful folk and they only ate berries."

"They were likely peaceful because they had killed everyone they didn't like!" Simon gasped, scaring himself at the thought of it.

"Do you know any of the funny words?" Benny asked in a pitch so high that dogs barked in the distance.

"Right! That's it! No more of this kind of talk!" Davy demanded. "It's time to go to sleep."

As they settled for the night, at Benny's insistence, they kept the battery lamp switched on inside the tent. After he drifted off to sleep, Simon switched it off and tried to get comfortable. As he too fell asleep, he thought about happy times like previous birthdays and Christmas experiences in a bid to leave no room in his dreams of Druids or Jack the Ripper.

"I hear something!" It was Benny, wide awake and screaming. "Where's the battery lamp? Who switched it off?"

"It's here somewhere," Simon muttered still half asleep. "What did you hear?"

"He was likely dreaming," Davy said dreamily. "Get back to sleep Benny and stop going on like a big baby!"

Just then, a strange sound came from the darkness outside the tent. It was indescribable but definitely not human. All four boys heard it this time and they all sat bolt upright, their breathing laboured, straining to listen.

Then it came again, only this time much louder. It was something like a snort coupled with heavy footsteps.

"It's the Ripper!" Benny screamed. "We are all for it! It's too dark for him to know we are just children!"

Simon rummaged frantically for the battery lamp, throwing jackets, food and sweaters out of the way. Suddenly he was aware of something pushing against the side of the tent, opposite to where the noise was coming from.

"We're surrounded!" he yelled. "There's something at this side as well!"

"It's the Druids!" Benny screamed hysterically. "I hate that Joe Watters!"

"It has to be them!" Rodney agreed. "If there's more than one because the Ripper worked alone! We are going to be slaughtered!"

Davy lost all pretence of courage and dived below whatever clothes he could find in search of the battery lamp. Amid the chaos and the noise of screams, he found it!

"Hold on till I put on the battery lamp!" he shouted, groping for the switch.

"No don't do that!" Rodney yelled. "If you do, and it's the Druids, they will see where we are and make us easier targets!"

"But if it's the Ripper," Benny wailed, "He won't know we are just children. Switch it on quick!"

And so it went. The battery lamp was on, then off, then on. The screaming continued and every time the lamp went on, it illuminated huge shapes outside the tent which increased the terror and the screaming. Eventually the old tent had had enough and collapsed on top of all four boys, causing mayhem as they each fought and scrambled to get out from below it. They mistook each other for evil druids or blood-thirsty nocturnal killers from the Victorian era. They pushed, shoved, kicked and punched until they were utterly exhausted, none of them having escaped from the canvas which by now had wrapped itself around them like a huge strait jacket.

The boys lay in silence, breathing deeply but hearing none of the terrible sounds or seeing none of the horrible shapes.

Tentatively, they unpicked themselves from the tangle of canvas and ropes and peered out from below it all, eight blinking eyes scanning the few metres around them.

"Maybe all the noise we made scared them away," Benny suggested hopefully.

"Well there's no one out there now," Davy said hesitantly.

Nervously they crept out and added a few more twigs to the embers of the fire. The dry twigs ignited quickly and they hurriedly added more branches, their confidence growing. As they sat staring wearily at the flames, they stopped suddenly. There it was again! That same noise! Altogether they looked around behind them, their hearts beating furiously. And there it was; the source of all their trouble!

As they stared into the darkness, a nosey black bullock stared back. Every now and again, the bullock snorted that same snort they had heard in the tent. The boys shone the beam of light towards the harmless beast and it responded by snorting loudly and ambling off into the darkness of the night.

The four said nothing initially but then Davy broke the silence.

"A bullock! All that commotion and the tent wrecked and all because of a bullock that's more scared of us than we were of it! It came over for a nosey and everyone suddenly believed Joe Watters's nonsense!"

"You believed it too, Davy," Simon said quietly. "We all did for a minute or two."

"What do we do now?" Benny asked.

"Well, the tent's wrecked," Rodney replied slowly. "Should we just head on home?"

No one spoke because no one had to. They got up wordlessly in unison and collected their belongings, pausing for a moment to kick dust over the dying fire.

"What about the tent?" Benny asked.

They all stopped and looked at the pile of canvas.

"Let it lie there," Davy replied. "We won't be needing it again."

Without another word, they turned and started off for home just as the sun began to arise over the horizon.

"Well, at least we done it, Druids and Rippers and all!" Simon said.

Despite themselves, they all laughed and headed towards the sun.

The Caravan

Pam Morris drank slowly from the cup of coffee as she flicked through the brochures, she had brought home from the Travel Agents. Bright photographs of sunny beaches, palm trees and white washed buildings looked back at her from the glossy pages. Pam imagined herself in each picture, lying on the beach, lounging by the pool or strolling along the cobbled streets. Then she looked at the other papers on the table; a bank statement that made dismal reading, an electric bill typed in red ink and a fine in the post for her husband who had driven through a red light. Pam closed the brochures and closed her eyes. What was the point in dreaming? There would be no foreign holidays this year or the next.

"What's all this junk?" Barry Morris demanded pointing vaguely in the direction of the brochures at teatime.

"Bills, bills and more bills," Pam replied. "Did you drive through a red light?"

"Never in my life," Barry answered firmly. "I don't mean that junk. I mean *that* junk!"

"Aw nothing," Pam sighed. "Just travel brochures. Just looking to see how the other half live. Nothing for you to worry about Barry as we are destined to stay in *this* half."

"I don't like foreign places," Barry said through a mouthful of potatoes and gravy. "That bright sun brings me out in a rash and no one in them places speaks English! And the food! Don't get me started! You don't know what you're eating!"

Pam looked despondently at Barry. She had heard these excuses a hundred times before and as Barry wolfed down the last of his tea, she knew eating out in a posh restaurant was also out of the question. Who could take Barry to a place where there was more than one knife and fork and where people didn't mop up their gravy with a heel of bread? She would be mortified! And imagine him when he gets the bill! She could just hear him and so would all the other customers too.

"So, where does that leave us?" Pam asked. "If we are to get a break, it must be somewhere where everyone speaks English, the sun isn't too strong and the food is something you can eat. Well done, Barry that discounts just about everywhere!"

"Well Pam, that's how it is. It's not my fault I have delicate skin and a dodgy stomach! Why do you need a break anyway? Sure your whole life is a holiday and you get to spend it with me!"

With that all said, Barry reclined in the chair and emitted a loud burp. He then smiled at his wife. "That was a great feed! Now what's on the TV the night?"

Pam watched wordlessly as her husband walked the short distance, from the table to the sofa, and threw himself down heavily on it. With remote control in hand, he rapidly punched the buttons looking for something to amuse himself until he would fall asleep where he sat. Welcome to my world, Pam thought. It's June and summer would be spent sitting on the lawn reading brochures about places other people would go in July and August.

A few days later when Barry was at work, Pam decided to have a browse through her local newspaper. Just the usual stuff, she thought. The odd burglary, a missing much-loved pet and profound promises from politicians. She was about to dispatch the newspaper to the recycling bin when something caught her eye. There in the classifieds section, she saw the answer to all her prayers; or an answer of sorts.

On an impulse, Pam lifted the receiver of her telephone and rang the number.

"Hello?" said the voice on the other end. "Who is this?"

"I am calling to see about the caravan you have for sale." Pam said nervously.

"Oh aye, it's for sale all right," said the voice. "It has been sitting at the side of our house for months now. My son sits in it for hours watching war movies. It's not healthy! It needs to go. Do you want it?"

Pam was surprised at this burst of needless information and the woman's insistence. Mind you, she thought, it sounds like she is desperate to sell so she might take less.

"Yes, I would be interested. Maybe. Can I call and view it? If you give me your address I can call this afternoon, if it's local."

The caravan owner seemed happy and relieved to have found a prospective buyer and gave her, her address, which Pam recognised as quite near her home. She reasoned that it was so near, she could go and see it within the hour if that suited the owner. The woman agreed and said she would have tea ready but instructed Pam to knock the kitchen window as opposed to the front door as her son was asleep upstairs. A bit cloak-and-dagger, Pam thought but she agreed nonetheless.

Fifty minutes after making that call, Pam arrived at the address and saw the caravan. It was in need of a good clean as it was parked beneath a huge tree which had left the roof and parts of the sides of it green. Pam sneaked a look inside and it seemed in reasonable condition though the empty beer cans and pizza boxes needed removed. Guessing which one was the kitchen window, Pam knocked the glass lightly. Suddenly the window flew open and a woman with a headscarf and huge eyes appeared from within.

"Ssshhh! Go easy, for goodness sake! You'll wake him up and then he'll know!"

Pam was literally taken aback and stepped away from the window immediately. Within seconds, the headscarf appeared at the corner of the house, complete with head and bulging eyes.

"Come on in through the back door quickly!" the headscarf clad face mouthed in a whisper.

This is like something out of a spy film, Pam thought as she followed the headscarf through the back door, almost tip toeing.

"Sorry for all this, but my son works at night and sleeps during the day. Between the two, he sits in that caravan watching war films and all kinds of violent nonsense. He's very impressionable and has convinced himself that the caravan is some kind of Headquarters where he controls all kinds of armies, spies and whatnot."

"What age is your son?" Pam asked expecting to be told around 18 years old.

"Thirty-two!" the woman exclaimed. Pam was momentarily in shock.

"Aye, and he has his problems. He spends far too much time on his own for a boy his age. Anyway, my name is Maud Watters. It's very nice to meet you. It's Sam isn't it? A strange name for a girl."

"Actually it's Pam, Mrs Watters. So how much did you say you need for the caravan?"

"Oh it's not *need*. I want 750 pounds. I don't need the money, but I need my Alfie to get out of World War II. He wanted to be a soldier, you see, but they didn't want him. I think that affected his mind."

"Would you take 700?" Pam asked, desperate to get out of this mad house. "If you take that for it, I will get my husband to tow it out, and all and I will take care of any rubbish inside it."

Maud Watters looked thoughtfully at Pam as if giving the offer the gravest of considerations.
"OK, Pam it's a deal. When can he lift it? It would be best to come when Alfie is at work. I will take out his junk, and his TV and DVD player. Aye, come when he's at work. Say 11 o'clock tomorrow night?"

Pam hurriedly excused herself and left the Watters home quietly. What a family!

When Barry came home from work, it was like Groundhog Day. His unbending consistency determined that he would eat his tea, complain and then watch TV until he fell asleep on the sofa. On this particular evening, he wolfed down the tea whilst venting his spleen about austerity, the cost of living and the ingratitude of people generally. There was never going to be a good time to tell his, she thought. It might as well be now.

"I think I have solved our holiday problem," she began hesitantly. "As you often said, you can't go anywhere too warm or you will have a rash; you can't go to places where they don't speak English, and you can't eat foreign food or you'll take a bad stomach."

Barry nodded vigorously as he ate the last forkful of food.

"Well then I have great news for you! We own a caravan!"

Barry stopped mid-chew, his moth wide open. Pam diverted her eyes to avoid the spectacle.

"We don't have the money for a caravan!" Barry spluttered, catching particles of food in a handkerchief.

"Ah, that's another thing," Pam said, rising from the table. "I managed to get a loan from the bank. They paid out straight away, and I took the money round to the owner just half an hour before you came home. We have to collect it this evening after 8pm."

Barry pushed his plate away as if he had lost his appetite completely. *A caravan???* He was aghast at the notion of sitting in a caravan on a wet week in the North Coast yet Pam had used all his arguments against him. He folded his arms and studied his wife as she impassively cleared away the dishes. He knew when he was beaten. He was now a shareholder in a caravan.

A month later, Pam looked around the caravan. The weather forecast for the next few days was good, and she had booked them into the caravan park on the north coast for five nights. Of course, Barry had complained of a sore back but that was predictable and ignored. She had bought tins of food, cup-a-soups and bread and had filled small canisters with tea, coffee and sugar with a tin of powdered milk for good measure. She checked and rechecked everything. Content, she went to the garage and struggled to pull the awning towards the car boot.

"We don't need that thing!" Barry bellowed from the doorstep. "There's only two of us going so that tent thing can stay in the garage."

Pam ignored him and shoved the awning into the boot, placing steel rods on the back seat of the car.

"That 'tent thing' as you call it is for us to sit in when it's evening, Barry. Just remember when we get to the caravan park, I packed it myself so you can put it up!"

The drive to the north coast was uneventful. As always, Barry impatiently switched from one radio station to another, scolding at the musical offerings available and getting angry at the content of political programmes. Pam flipped through her bag of books and magazines, imagining herself sitting reading to the faint noise of the sea lapping against the rocks. This will be a nice relaxing wee break for me; and infuriating for Barry, she thought mischievously.

When they drove into the caravan park, Pam looked at the different vehicles and made brief judgements on them. Too big, too small, too flashy, too old. They parked up at their allotted spot and Barry manfully unhooked the caravan despite his supposed backache. Pam then sent him for water as she sorted out the few bits and pieces that had fallen on the way there.

"Well!" Barry gasped. "That was a bit of a hike for water! Pour me a glass of it, Pam. I feel a bit weak after that adventure!"

"Did you see the folk in the caravan next to us?" Pam asked, ignoring Barry's dramatics. "They seem like nice people."

Barry peered out of the window. A huge woman sat on a folding chair breathing heavily. She wore sunglasses even though it was quite cloudy and sipped a glass of wine. A thin, balding man whom Barry guessed to be her husband then joined her, looking at the sky but not speaking. *How do you know by just looking at someone if they're nice*? Barry wondered.

"Are you recovered enough to put the awning up?" Pam asked as she prepared sandwiches for them. "Away you go there and get it up while I make us a bite to eat."

Barry heaved the canvas from the boot of the car and the poles from the back seat and spread it all out on the grass. He stared at it all totally mystified.

"Was there not a diagram came with this or some kind of instructions?" he yelled at his wife.

"Barry, stop all the drama and just put it up," she replied exasperated.

Barry set about the task with a distinct lack of enthusiasm. He struggled to find the end he needed to begin the attachment to the caravan but failed miserably. He found himself standing on the parts he was trying to lift and getting all the more irritated by this shapeless mass of canvas.

"Can I help you?" A voice said from behind him. Barry looked around and saw the thin man from the next caravan. "My name is Ronnie Spence," he added offering his hand. Sweating and puffing, Barry took the hand. "Barry," he wheezed.

Within the next 20 minutes, Barry and John had the awning erected, albeit with a pole missing but Barry reckoned it would do rightly without it as it *looked* like other awnings around them. Well almost anyway. Pam brought out tea and sandwiches and asked John to fetch his wife to join them. Madge Spence came puffing around the side of the caravan, carrying her chair, placed it in the shade and sat down heavily.

"This is lovely," Pam enthused as Barry mopped the sweat from his brow. "The sound of the sea, the sun shining and birds singing."

"Not many pigeons about mind you," Ronnie observed. "They're all seagulls, as far as I can see."

"Ignore him," Madge said wearily. "He has a thing about pigeons. We had to leave our son John in charge of his pigeons at home, and he has fretted about them since we arrived here. It's the same every time we come here and we have been coming here for 5 years now."

They spoke about their lives and Barry especially was surprised to learn that this odd couple had apparently bred a son who was a hero, having foiled a robbery and a joy rider. There was nothing in this Ronnie and Madge to suggest that they could have produced such a child. Barry focussed on his work in the motor industry and the importance of it whilst being vague on detail, being in reality a traffic warden.

It started to get cool when the sun set and Pam suggested they should move inside the caravan, but Madge thanked her and said it had been a long day and her and Ronnie would be having an early night and took their leave. Pam and Barry then folded the chairs and retired indoors.

Madge tidied their caravan as Ronnie prepared for bed. We need a new one, Madge thought morosely. This caravan is as old as the hills and the whole way up here it swung all over the road. The floor creaked beneath her weight as she puffed loudly, bending down to lift a newspapers and tidy shoes discarded earlier. I'm sure Ronnie will find some reason to hang on to this jalopy for another year, she thought, glaring at her benign husband as he stared happily out of the window at the darkness. What a man! What an excuse for a husband!

Ronnie enjoyed the caravan but didn't enjoy the sleeping arrangements. The bed was far too narrow for both of them. He lay on his side as Madge tossed and turned and groaned loudly in a bid to find a comfortable sleeping position. Ronnie hoped their son John was keeping an eye on the pigeons. You never know with the cats on their street. They were vicious killers. Ronnie shivered at the thought of it and drifted off to sleep to the soft patter of light rain falling on the roof.

Suddenly Ronnie's world was literally upside down. A loud crash coincided with a sudden movement that smashed the sleeping Ronnie into his wife's back. In the darkness, utter confusion reigned. Madge yelled out in panic and fear as Ronnie scrambled to get to his feet and failed. Madge's yells became mournful wails and Ronnie was in total confusion. He made one last desperate bid to get to his feet and this time, after a lot of effort and despite Madge's grabbing his arm and pulling him back down, Ronnie made it. He stumbled to the light switch and looked back to where he came from. The sight that beheld him was truly amazing and shocking! The whole caravan appeared to have capsized to the right! The front end of the caravan was only slightly tilted but the back end was completely collapsed. He almost laughed out loud when he saw the carnage before him. Madge, her hair in rollers, was looking up at him from below the duvet, her left arm propping her up at a most bizarre angle. Where he had been sleeping, the bed was high but at Madge's side, it seemed level with the ground.

"What has happened?" Madge asked, her eyes wide with alarm. "Has the ground subsided or has there been an earthquake?"

Ronnie simply had no answers. He turned silently from his bedraggled wife and stepped outside. What he saw next baffled and amazed him. The caravan was lying completely to one side! He quickly retrieved a torch from the caravan, ignoring the demands from his lopsided wife who still lay half in and half out of the bed bewildered at this turn of events. On closer inspection, Ronnie discovered what he already suspected; the axle had broken and the caravan wheel lay uselessly at the side of the caravan. He closed his eyes for a moment and then went back inside the caravan to rescue Madge.

After a lot of effort and the use of some very colourful language, Ronnie managed to heave Madge out of the bed and onto her feet and they stood at an angle staring at each other, sweating and breathless.

"I am saying nothing!" Madge declared loudly. "What would be the point? You have known for months there was something wrong with that wheel and what did you do? Nothing! And now look at us!"

"That's a lot of words for someone who had nothing to say." Ronnie replied irritably.

Madge looked at Ronnie with surprise and shock. She would like him to be a bit more assertive but this was neither the time nor the place! She silently hobbled out of the stricken vehicle and looked at the damage as Ronnie stood behind her surprised at his robust retort.

"Is everything all right?" a voice in the darkness asked, sounding like Pam next door.

"Well, not really," Ronnie stammered, back to his old unsure self. "The caravan has collapsed a bit."

"A *bit*?" Madge declared loudly. "It's scrap value, is what it is!"

"Just wait there and we will be out in a tick," Pam shouted.

"What's all the shouting about?" Barry asked sleepily.

"Ronnie and Madge next door," Pam replied. "Looks like their caravan has collapsed."

"I'm not surprised!" Barry said more alert. "The size of that woman and the age of the caravan. It's a bad mix! Anyway what can we do about it? I'm not a welder and if has collapsed it will be because the axle has gone south. Anyway, it's lashing out there."

"Well we need to do something!" Pam insisted pulling on a jacket. "Up you get and help me out."

In a few minutes, Barry was standing beside the caravan in the rain, looking ridiculous in nothing but his boxers and an overcoat. They surveyed the scene and exchanged a few words before adjourning to Barry and Pam's caravan to get dried out and have some hot tea.

"Well, we can't lie in that heap the night!" Madge observed angrily. "We may find a hotel and spend the rest of the night in it until we see if we can get the caravan fixed."

"There's no need for that," Pam replied quickly. "You can have our bed!"

Barry choked on his cigarette and stared wildly at his wife, coughing loudly.

"Where are we going to sleep?" he demanded, breathless at the coughing fit.

"Out in the awning, dear," Pam said patiently.

"I'm not for sleeping in any tent!" Barry exclaimed. "You know rightly the damp air plays havoc with my chest. Of course, I would like to help but sleeping in that tent is out of the question!"

"Stop making a show of yourself, dear," Pam said smiling. "Ignore my Barry. He's always so dramatic. We would be only too happy to give you our bed and we will be quite content in the awning." Looking at Barry, she added, "The awning, dear, not a tent. And we will love it. It might actually be quite romantic."

Barry felt a mixture of rage and embarrassment. Obviously, he couldn't argue with Pam in front of Ronnie and Madge who were sitting there looking pitiful. They were wet and miserable and Barry, who wasn't all bad, reluctantly agreed with his wife.

"Well, of course I am only winding Pam up," he said by way of explanation for his earlier outburst. "I will just get the spare duvet out of the cupboard and we'll let you get some sleep."

When they were in the awning, out of earshot, Barry made his feelings known.

"We have to sleep on the groundsheet! You know what my back is like and by the morning I will likely not be able to stand up straight. And the rain is still beating down on the roof of this tent! I will never sleep the night! It's all very well for that pair in there, lying in a nice comfortable bed that we warmed up for them but us out here! I give up! If I had known we would have to sleep out here I would have bought us a tent!"

"Are you done?" Pam asked, inwardly laughing at Barry's tirade. "We are doing the right thing. They are a lot older than us and sure it's only for one night. Sleep well, pet."

Barry couldn't believe it when, seconds later, he heard Pam's breathing change, signifying that she was fast asleep. He tossed and turned but to no avail. The rain was definitely getting heavier outside and the patter he had heard in the caravan had become a heavy drumming noise on the roof of the tent. Barry sighed loudly and sat up, pulling a cigarette out of the packet and inhaled deeply, exhaling noisily. He wondered if the missing steel pole had been misplaced or was it in the car or maybe it had fell out somewhere.

As he was musing on the whereabouts of the elusive pole, Barry suddenly heard what sounded like a tearing noise. Instinctively he looked up at the sagging roof and before he knew what was happening, the canvas parted and a deluge of water poured in on top of him and his sleeping wife.

Pam awoke screaming in shock and looked at Barry wide-eyed. Barry was struggling to get out from below the duvet, holding his right hand away from himself in a bid to protect his cigarette. She could see that Barry was completely soaked down one side and wore a look of dishevelled exasperation. She then looked up and saw the rain pouring in a long slit in the canvas.

"Now we know where the missing pole was meant to be," she advised Barry helpfully.

"When I agreed to go in the caravan, I actually believed we would be sleeping *in* the caravan," Barry began evenly before raising his voice to a shout. "But I did not expect to be sitting here at this hour of the night ringing wet while total strangers lie nice and snug in *my* bed!"

Pam got up slowly in the full knowledge that, like a volcano, Barry would appear calm on the outside whilst boiling inside with the inevitable eruption only moments away. Silently, she tiptoed past her volatile husband towards the door of the caravan.

"I am just getting on my jogging bottoms and shoes," Pam said quietly. "Can you get started fixing that (pointing to the tear) and I will be out again in a wee minute."

Barry stared silently as his wife then entered the caravan, closing the door quietly behind her. He took another drag of his cigarette and squinted up at the tear. There was masking tape in the boot of the car, he thought. Maybe I can patch the tear temporarily and get us through the night. He flicked his cigarette beyond him and peeled back the soggy duvet. Staring at the rip in the canvas as he walked, Barry did not notice the faint yet angry glow of his cigarette butt. However, when his bare foot stepped down as he approached the exit of the awning, he soon remembered it! The burning cigarette end bored into his foot as he stepped heavily on it, sticking to his foot as he raised it. Barry screamed and yelled in pain and despair as the butt burned deeper into his sole. He kicked and thrashed and hopped frantically in a futile bid to shake the butt off his tormented foot. He reached down and hit it with his fingers and watched in relief as it flew harmlessly through the air and landed on the iron step into the caravan to burn out.

The pain in his foot was excruciating as he rubbed it frantically along the wet grass in a bid to soothe it. *Where on earth has that Pam got to?* he wondered angrily as the dripping water ran irritatingly down his back. This is the worst night of my life! He stumbled across the wet groundsheet to the door of the caravan and flung it open. He couldn't believe his eyes! There was Pam lying on the makeshift sofa covered by a coat asleep!

Barry slammed the door shut and went to the car. He sat in the driver's seat and switched on the ignition, putting the heating on fully. It was freezing air to begin with but then heated up. He put the window down a few millimetres and reclined his seat. For once in his entire words, Barry was lost for words! He switched on the radio and thought of a week in Spain as an orchestra played through the speakers and he drifted off to an exhausted sleep.

In his sleep, Barry heard a light tapping sound. Momentarily disoriented, he opened his eyes and blinked hard for a few seconds. He was in his car? Then he remembered the fiasco of the night before and wiped condensation from the glass with his hand to see Pam standing. He wound down the window fully and stared at her.

"Good morning, sleepy head," she gushed. "Ronnie and Madge are away to get someone to sort out their caravan and I have made coffee." She reached him his cup and he took it stiffly. "They won't be back for an hour or so." Barry drained the lukewarm cup of coffee in one gulp.

"An hour, you say?" he repeated. "Right, get packed because we are for home!"

Pam was genuinely surprised. But, without further ado, Barry was out of the car and hitching the caravan to the tow bar. Pam hurriedly folded up what was left of the awning and threw it roughly into the caravan and within twenty-five minutes of waking Barry, they were in the car driving home. Barry seemed to have something on his mind and then, after half an hour he spoke.

"How much was a week in Spain for two in them brochures you had?" he asked suddenly.

"Oh, roughly what we paid for the caravan," Pam replied wonderingly.

"Right then! As soon as we get home, get that thing sold and look at them brochures again. When you see one for that price, book it! We're going abroad and I will never be in a caravan again!"

"Anything you say, dear." Pam said, looking out of the passenger window. And then she smiled widely.

The People's Choice

It was a quiet Saturday morning in the Copper Jug cafe. Pensioners sat in small groups around spotless tables sharing a pot of tea and items of gossip. Somewhere at the back, a baby protested about the portions the mother was feeding him and heads turned briefly to see the source of the noise before returning to their huddles of indecipherable whispers. In the front, by the window, three young men sat quietly. One was studying the local newspaper, periodically shaking his head and gasping elaborately as if unable to believe some of the content. Phil Redmond had been convening this Saturday morning meeting with his friends Steve Rollins and Mike Jackson for months now. It was uncanny how rigid their routine seemed to be. Each week, Phil read the weekly newspapers and wound himself up into elaborate rages; whilst Steve sought to be a calming influence and Mike happily ignored the other two, preferring to listen to music being pumped through a set of earphones.

These three had been friends since primary school and in all that time they had never really fallen out. They had differences of opinion in that Phil was quick and loud to express his opinions, whereas Steve normally had an opposite one and Mike appeared to have no opinions at all. Phil was the kind of person who would eventually seise control of a small nation and rule as a despot for the rest of his life. It wasn't that he was cruel; he just believed he knew best regardless of the views of others. Steve wasn't as loud or as eager to express his opinions but he had his own ideas about things and expressed them in his own quiet way. Mike found it best to ignore Phil and tolerate Steve. He had his own thoughts on many matters but he saw no point in adding fuel to the fire by expressing them. Pearls before swine, he thought at the idea of talking sense to these two. He chuckled as the '80s music filled his ears and his mind.

"OUTRAGEOUS!" Phil suddenly roared, thumping the table with his fist, causing some tea spillage. People gasped in shock at the outburst which had been so loud that Mike has also heard it above the sound of Gary Numan. Old Mrs Briggs clutched her heart and looked frightened, grabbing a friend with her free hand as if to get reassurance that the shout had not killed her outright. The baby at the back squealed in terror and could not be pacified regardless of the mother's best efforts and repeatedly making a hissing sound. The women from the Ladies Bowling Club were not so easily frightened and glared angrily at the trio muttering words of insult and using adjectives children should not hear.

"What is it?" Steve gasped when he had settled down after the initial shock.

"Rates! They have put them up again! In this town, the councillors are all for the rich and they just treat the poor and the working class like dirt. DIRT!"

His loud repeat of the last word attracted a few more angry looks and led to the departure of old Mrs Briggs and her aged companion.

"And what can you do about it? Apart from scaring pensioners," Steve asked, watching old Mrs Briggs and her pal shuffle out of the Copper Jug to a place of safety where a quiet ambience could be enjoyed.

"Here you!" cried Muriel who worked at the counter. "No more of that shouting or you're out of here!"

"Oh really?" Phil retorted; his face contorted in fury. "Why? So you can give these seats to the rich maybe? I'm surprised at you Muriel!"

"No, Phil," Muriel replied sighing, "But I might give them to 'paying' customers. That pot of tea you bought an hour ago for two quid won't save me from the poverty you're always on about."

"Ah, a refill is required I think!" Phil announced, ignoring Muriel. "Go on, Mike, get them in. It's your shout."

Mike looked at Phil and Steve with a look of exasperation. The exertion of having to walk to the counter added to the prospect of another hour of nonsense from Phil seemed to engulf him in a mixture of dread and deep depression. Phil stared back with determination and cocked one eyebrow as if to ask why he wasn't way for the teas. Mike then sagged his shoulders in defeat and left to make his purchases.

Phil then nudged Steve roughly, "I also read that the summer seats in the park are being removed due to increased vandalism and anti-social behaviour. Well, we all know what that's really all about!"

Steve gave Phil a baffled look and offered his palm indicating that the political animal should continue.

"Well it's obvious! The council doesn't want the old folk, the young folk or any folk at all sitting out in public areas! Their simple lives are an embarrassment to the political elite so they are taking the seats away to keep them in their homes! And, of course, they won't have to pay to varnish the seats so they will save money there and that money will be plundered by the councillors to pay for their expenses! AND they blame the young folk, making them scapegoats for their devious plans!"

"Do you really believe all that?" Steve asked in obvious disbelief.

"One thing about our Phil is that he believes 'everything' he says," Mike offered as he placed the teapot and clean cups before them before sitting down and unplugging his ears. "And he believes it because he also believes that everything he says is right. Remember at primary school when the teacher asked someone to name the four seasons? Phil put his hand up and said he couldn't name them individually but he could name a few of their songs!"

Phil glared at Mike who was laughing happily at the memory.

"And then when the teacher said, 'not the pop group', you said OK then, that's easy; salt, pepper, vinegar and sage!"

Phil looked all around the cafe to see if anyone might have heard that and then leaned across to Mike who was slipping off his chair in hysterics.

"It's all very well you sitting there sniggering! You just don't care. Anyway, what the teacher said that day was open to interpretation. In a way, I was actually right. Anyway, get them teas poured and let's get out of here!"

The three drank their teas quickly and left, much to the relief of Muriel and other customers who simply wanted a quiet bite to eat.

Phil Redmond was always something of a fantasist, written off by many as a harmless idiot. It was said that the strain of insanity that spurred on his wild ideas, and non-stop planning and scheming stemmed from his mother's family. She was a Belfast woman, Isobel Watters, who met and married Phil's dad, John Redmond back in the '60s. Isobel was an unusual woman in that she exaggerated every single thing. If Isobel had seen an airplane cross the skies above her, she would tell people she saw two and they almost collided. If Isobel developed a mild cold, she would be at A&E demanding immediate treatment for fear it may be an unknown and highly contagious virus. Even when diagnosed with the harmless common cold, she would 'claim' to have that very same virus. Older people recalled a brother coming to stay for a while with Isobel and John. Alfie Watters wreaked havoc around the town during his sojourn there with his endless lies, fables and general idiocy. When he left, the older folk agreed that, that's where Phil got his foolishness from. As they walked down the main street that bright Saturday morning, Steve flinched with embarrassment as Phil waved and shouted brash salutations at just about everyone he met. Mike noticed smugly that quite a few tended to take sudden interest in shop windows as Phil approached but that didn't deter him from making himself known to them. At the bottom of the street, Phil stopped abruptly and seemed to be lost in concentration as he stared straight ahead at a piece of wasteland facing them.

"I don't believe it!" he exclaimed. "Look at that!"

The other two glanced at the wasteland without comment. It had lain like that for the last eighteen years and hadn't changed at all. Surely even Phil couldn't pretend to have not noticed it all before. They had even played in the wasteland as children only a few years ago!

"What is it we are looking at, Phil?" Mike asked seriously.

"That eyesore! What is that all about? It has lain like that for donkey's years and it is an absolute DISGRACE! Where are our councillors? Where is the MP for here? Why has that eyesore not been developed and turned into affordable housing or made into a recreation area for our young folk?"

"As to the whereabouts of the councillors and MP, I admit that I have no idea where they are but as it's a Saturday morning, they might be doing something enjoyable and relaxing instead of acting surprised at something that isn't surprising and being put on edge by a yelling maniac! As to your third question, likely because there's no money to do any of those things."

Steve couldn't help but imagine the wasteland being transformed into neat cottages or maybe a grassy park with a water feature. It was a nice idea but neither of them would accomplish the task, no matter how much Phil believed in himself.

"One of these days, I will make changes," Phil muttered to himself. "The folk of this town will know the name of Phil Redmond and they will be grateful!"

Steve and Mike glanced at each other with raised eyebrows and rolling eyes. Then they parted company so Mike could get another hour's sleep and Steve could prepare for a football match; whilst Phil prepared himself for greatness.

A week passed and the friends hadn't the opportunity to see each other but that changed monumentally on the Friday evening. Steve had just finished his tea when the house seemed to shake with the force of a loud banging on the front door. Steve and his parents looked at each other in surprise. Who could be attacking their door with such aggression? Steve's father tentatively looked out of the living room window to ascertain the cause of the continuing banging.

"It's that head case Phil Redmond! Away out there and tell him to knock that thumping on the head or I will go out there and thump him!"

Immediately Steve leapt from his chair and ran towards the front door, feeling guilty and awkward that he was indirectly responsible for the fuss and ado that had caused his mild-mannered father to threaten violence if it did not stop immediately.

When he opened the door, he almost took a knock from Phil's fist which seemed to have taken on a life of its own as a mini battering ram.

"What's the matter with you?" Steve demanded, pushing Phil backwards and closing the door behind him. "Is your head clean away with it? My da is raging in there! I hope you didn't chip the paint on that door or he will have a fit!"

"Never mind all that!" Phil bellowed, caring neither for Steve's father or the front door. "You will never ever believe this! Old John McMullan is dead!"

Steve had no idea who the late John McMullan was but it was clear that Phil welcomed the old man's death for some reason. Steve shrugged his shoulders and offered his upturned palms to indicate bewilderment, both at the news and at Phil's apparent joy.

"McMullan!" Phil yelled; his frustration visible in his scowling face. "The ancient councillor who kept falling asleep during meetings! Well he's not waking up from this one! He's dead and gone!"

"Oh aye, I heard about the one who falls asleep!" Steve replied, realisation dawning on him. "I never knew his name but I heard about him, all right. And what, though? Did you know him?"

Phil stared at Steve as if he was insane and had just asked the silliest question ever put forward.

"No, I did not!" Phil snapped. "I don't have to 'know him' to know he was an independent councillor so that means there will have to be a by-election!"

Steve looked blankly at Phil. He understood that the death of a councillor would mean a by-election but so what? He waited on Phil to finish his story.

"Don't stand there looking stupid, Steve! If there's a by-election then there needs to be a candidate who will win! A good man who knows what the 'people' want!"

"Maybe a good woman?" Steve suggested, missing Phil's point completely, or letting on to miss it.

Phil stared at his friend. Was Steve really this stupid? Could he really not see the point in all of this? Did he really need it spelt out to him?

"Me!" Phil bellowed. "The council needs ME! The folk of the area need ME! I am the answer! Now grab your coat and come on!"

"You?" Steve asked, his eyebrows raised in genuine surprise. "Are you sure, Phil? Like, I know you heart is in the right place but do you think voters know that?"

Phil sighed as if exasperated. "That's what election campaigns are about, dimwit! By the time the actual election comes, everyone will know that Phil Redmond is the man! Now come on!"

"Where are we going?" Steve asked with apprehension. Surely we aren't for old McMullan's wake?

"To get Mike. I know he's useless but he will have to do. He doesn't actually have to speak to folk. He can be in charge of posters and leaflets and the like. That way he can keep plugged into his music and the exercise will do him good. I have noticed Jacko has put on a bit of weight lately."

Good old Phil, Steve thought, pulling on his coat. He's always thinking of others. Jacko, the name by which Mike had always been known, is poster paster and leaflet dropper in order to help him lose weight and increase fitness. Steve often wondered if Phil really believed he was always working for the good of others or was it a cynical ploy to get the help he needed. With Phil, it was hard to know!

When Mike heard the news, he replied by way of a stunned silence and a bemused look on his face. Phil Redmond was running for the council? Phil Redmond who famously said in school that Hadrian's Wall was built by brickies on minimum wage therefore folk should boycott it. Phil Redmond who recently blasted a local councillor for saying that the green belt must be protected. Back then Phil had stormed that no one had any right to tell a rate payer how to hold up his trousers. Phil thought it outrageous that a green belt should get special protection and stated that speaking for himself, he preferred braces anyway. Jacko and Steve had thought he was joking and had laughed but they were met with a glare from Phil that told them he was serious.

"You need a proposer, a seconder and eight others to sign your nomination papers," Mike said blandly, as if offering a challenge.

"Well that won't be too hard," Phil replied. "There's you two for a start. One can propose and the other can second. Then we can think about another eight after that."

"You seriously think you will find eight people who would be happy to nominate you as a candidate?" Mike asked in genuine shock. "Where would you find eight folks as daft as me and Steve?"

Phil grimaced and pulled out a writing pad and two biro pens. He began to list possible signatories and areas where posters would be needed. He then flipped over a few pages and began to write his election literature. Now and again he asked his friends for their opinions but more often than not, he ignored their suggestions. Finally, after about two hours, Phil set the pen down and leaned back on his chair, cupping both his hands behind his head.

"We are on a winner, boys!" he announced triumphantly. "I can just feel it in my water!"

The other two looked at each other and then looked at Phil. They could see that he was present only in body and that his mind was already racing from one place to another, far away from where they sat. He may come across as insane at times, but they were both in awe of Phil's belief in himself. He had an amazing capacity to believe every word he spoke and in his own infallibility.

A few days later, the word came through that there would indeed be a by-election and the date was set for three weeks from that date. Phil was in top gear when he summoned Mike and Steve to the Copper Jug for a 'planning meeting'. They sat sharing a pot of tea and Phil explained that he had already presented his manifesto to a local printer and, having sold his motorbike and with the help of a credit union loan, he had enough cash on hand to pay for the leaflets and the posters. When asked about advertisements in local papers, Phil replied with cunning that he was going to bombard the papers with lengthy letters and offer himself up for interviews. These would not require payments of any kind. He added that if he was able to win a council seat on a minute budget, just think of what he could do if he got his hands on the rates!

In no time at all, Phil arrived with Steve at Mike's home. Steve's dad's car had somehow become the campaign wagon and Mike was instructed to open the boot of the car and look in the back seat as well.

"There you go, Jacko!" Phil said happily, pointing to a pile of election posters in the boot and then thousands of black and white leaflets in the back seat. "You know your duty here, son! Get the posters up and the leaflets out!"

Mike stared at the array of papers before him.

"Please don't make up any election soundbites or catch phrases, mate," he said, clearly disapproving of Phil's crisp manner. "Like, you do want to get elected, don't you?"

Steve shrugged his shoulders. "Maybe it would be best to let the leaflets do the talking, right enough. Sure it's all there? You have nothing to add?"

"'All there? Nothing to add?' Are you bonkers?" Phil roared. "That's only headings and wee bits and pieces! I have plenty more to say!"

The next two weeks were non-stop election work. Steve held the ladder as Mike climbed up and affixed Phil's smiling face to the lampposts. Mike believed that Phil's forced smile made him look like a serial killer and would thus, seriously lose him votes but neither of them had the heart to mention it to Phil who saw himself as a Churchillian type, shouting hello at anyone and everyone. Steve's dad was unhappy to find Phil's smiling face staring at him from the drivers and passenger's doors as well as along the bonnet.

"What's wrong with that lad?" he demanded from Steve. "He looks constipated in that poster!"

Again, this was feedback the candidate could do without, Steve reasoned, assuring his dad that the posters would be removed the minute the polls closed on election day. Not a minute too soon as it turned out because one day soon after that, as Steve, Mike and Phil were walking along the street, a young girl pointed at them and screamed to her mother,

"Look mummy! It i's the scary man from the posters!"

Thankfully, Phil preferred to have heard it as the 'very man from the posters'. In response, he smiled and waved, shouting his customary 'Hello!' as the little girl cowered in fear.

Phil's letters to the local press had mixed reactions. His ideas about developing areas and derelict buildings were highly commendable but hardly the remit of a local councillor. His attacks on the 'capitalist' system and the plight of a weary working class were also well received by many. The fact that most of Phil's ideas and plans were a mixed bag of pipe dreams and wishful thinking seemed to be more and more irrelevant to the ordinary voter. Suddenly Steve could detect an element of cunning in Phil's campaign. He discussed his theory on Phil with Mike as they put up the last of the posters.

"Jacko, I think Phil is either completely mad or he is being very clever. His ideas are appealing and what every politician worth their salt would like to achieve but they are totally unrealistic. Yet, as I read his letters and interviews, even I can't help thinking 'Go for it, Phil!' Now if I think like that and I know him, what about the public out there who don't know him? They will think he's just what the doctor ordered! More play areas for children, more public facilities, better roads, cleaner streets, lower rates and all that. Like, one contradicts the other! He wants to spend millions on the one hand but cut the rates on the other! It doesn't make sense when you look into it yet on the face of it, his ideas are just what the people want. I actually think he will get votes!"

"Steve, I have more news for you on that," Mike said as he rested against his ladder. "Folk are warming to him. I have spoken to loads of folk who asked me to pass on their best and told me they will be voting for him. Folk don't care about the nitty gritty of it all. They just want what he says he will get them and he's the only one either mad enough or cute enough to promise it. And he's smarter than we think because he's already preparing the ground for when he fails to get all these things. I read in the paper that another candidate has said his ideas are ridiculous and unobtainable but our Phil came back saying that just proves that the other candidates don't want to give the people what they want! He is as cute as a fox, that boy!"

The next day, one week before the by-election, Phil called with Steve before seven in the morning. Again, he managed to irk Steve's dad who came stumbling in to awake his son.

"You better get up. Tony Benn is here to see you."

Steve rushed up and let Phil in to the house and as usual he began his talking before he had taken his first step indoors.

"Right, listen to me and don't panic!" Phil gasped.

"That alone makes me panic!" Steve replied, fearing the worst.

"We—as in the election candidates—will be having a live debate in the town hall in a couple of days! Like, we're talking two days before the actual election!"

Steve's heart sank. The very idea of Phil publicly debating issues and matters of interest to an unsuspecting electorate two days before the election was anathema! There could be no hiding Phil's annoying ways and distinct lack of knowledge about local politics. The other candidates would have a field day! Steve looked open-mouthed and silent at his grinning friend as these thoughts tumbled through his mind. Phil then launched into a full tirade of what he would say, what his opponents might say in response and the possible re-action of the audience. It was all too much for Steve who suddenly 'remembered' that he had somewhere to go. Phil was fine about that and Steve watched with increasing despair as his friend marched down the avenue, talking away to himself and gesticulating wildly. Imagine if people are watching, Steve thought glumly. As soon as Phil was out of sight, Steve rang Mike with the news. Instead of the stunned silence and terror Steve experienced on hearing the news, Mike exploded into guffaws of laughter. In fact, Steve had to shout to be heard and became very irritated when his friend laughed even louder as the conversation continued.

"Oh, I can just see it!" Phil gasped between peals of laughter. "Phil, talking about global warming and the plight of the Asian elephant as the others discuss rated, public amenities and the problem of dog fouling! It will be priceless! I definitely want a front row seat for that one, Steve!"

Steve set the phone down and surmised that Mike probably hadn't noticed he had done so. He wished he could be like Jacko, the jolly one, who loved to laugh and take life not at all seriously. The public debate was going to be a disaster and, of the three of them, Steve felt that he was the only one who could see it.

On the evening of the public debate, Steve waited nervously on the steps of the town hall as the good citizens of the borough filed in past. Phil was all smiles in a pressed suit, greeting everyone with a frightening smile and loud words of salutation. The other candidates were in their seats waiting patiently and making strained small talk amongst themselves but not Phil Redmond. As the others glanced disparagingly at the empty seat on the stage, Phil continued on his charm offensive on the town hall steps until the compere insisted that he would take his seat to allow the proceedings to begin.

Waiting on the wings behind a curtain, Steve could see a healthy crowd filling the seats downstairs and even a few in the gallery. As he had promised, Mike Jackson was sitting smiling cheerfully in the front row, eager for the whole thing to start.

The first item of the night was for each candidate to describe in turn what meant most to them and which issues they intended to pursue above all others. The other three candidates rolled out what had been in their manifestos, each receiving polite but muted applause from the voters. When it was Phil's turn, he launched into a full attack on just about every decision the council had made in the past 20 years. He lambasted the 'lack of interest' of councillors that had led to the closure of some shops and businesses; listing most of them and counting them off on his fingers as he did so. Luckily for Phil, there were quite a few elderly voters in the audience who remembered these long-gone shops and businesses and this recognition led many of them to clap as he named each one. Encouraged by this, Phil grew even more animated and when he had exhausted his list, he demanded to know how many folks had been left unemployed after these closures. He asked where had the money these businesses had generated gone? No one ventured to answer his questions but the crowd was for Phil and clapped loudly, calling out and demanding answers from the other agitated candidates. Steve was stunned at the reaction and when he looked at Mike, he was holding his hand over his mouth trying to stifle his giggles.

When asked what each candidate proposed to do to improve the fortunes of the town, the other candidates were careful, stressing the importance of spending public money sensibly. Phil however, had no such reservations. He said it was a disgrace that so many derelict buildings were 'blotting the landscape' and that there were 'acres of waste land' that could be converted into public places for the elderly, unemployed and youth to enjoy. Phil reasoned that as the council had sat back and allowed the unemployed to lose their jobs, it was only right that they gave them somewhere to go. Also, he argued, the youth wouldn't be as inclined to be involved in muggings, graffiti and general anti-social behaviour if they had somewhere to go and something to do. The fact that the youth of the town weren't involved in these activities to any extent was irrelevant to Phil. The applause from the crowd justified his comments. The other candidates, fearing that they were losing ground, attacked the reckless plans Phil had for spending the rates but Phil countered by accusing them of not caring about 'the ordinary folk' and 'thinking the rates money was their own'. He then turned to the crowd and challenged them to show their distaste for the 'mean spirited candidates on his left'. Immediately the crowd responded, hurling abuse at the other candidates and venting their wrath. Phil then held up his hands to settle his followers and simply asked the crowd if they found him an acceptable candidate to which he received rapturous applause and loud cheers! Steve was totally dumbfounded and even Mike looked shocked as he scanned the crowd around him! Phil beamed and bowed like a maestro.

Two days later, the election was held. The feedback from the debate had been amazing and Steve couldn't believe the response from voters as he stood canvassing at the various school gates. It looked as if Phil was actually going to be in the running. That night, as Phil held court outside the largest polling station just after it closed, Steve sat on a convenient kerb and asked Mike for his opinion.

"I thought this was going to be a fiasco, but now I am not so sure," Steve mused. "I can't believe how things have turned out. I actually think he has a chance of winning the seat!"

"Listen, Steve," Mike responded. "Phil is either mad or bad. I have never been sure which and I've known him all my life. That public debate was something else. He hasn't a clue but he was crafty enough to play to the crowd. The others had more sense and they all know a thing or two about local politics but Phil is far too smart for them. He told the folk what they wanted to hear! It doesn't matter if it works or not. He doesn't have to 'prove' anything until after the election. What kind of a councillor will he be? Who knows? But if I know Phil Redmond, he will always come out of every situation smelling of roses!"

The next day, the count ended and the candidates lined up to hear the results. They were called out alphabetically which meant that Phil was the last candidate. The poll had been low and as the votes for each candidate was announced, Steve and Mike waited nervously. Phil was also counting and estimating, his beaming smile reduced to a nervous grimace as each candidate heard their result.

Atkins, Ulster Unionist, 134 votes

Boyle, Sinn Fein, 130 votes
Ferguson, Alliance, 101 votes
Peterson, Democratic Unionist, 132 votes
Redmond, Independent, 479 votes.

Phil looked totally shocked and immediately turned to his friends who responded with looks of even greater shock, if that were possible. Not only had Phil won but it had been a landslide! After a brief stunned silence, Mike lead the cheering and clapping and Phil jumped from the low stage and ran to hug his pals. They then ran for the door and the waiting public looked expectantly at their champion.

"I won by a landslide! And if I won, then YOU have won!"

The crowd went mad, clapping and cheering and before Phil knew it, a couple of sturdy unemployed meat packers grabbed him and roughly placed him on their shoulders, carrying through the crowd as Phil reached down to shake hands and slap skin.

Mike and Steve watched in awe of their fanatical friend. They looked at each other blankly then looked back at the spectacle before them.

"There he goes," observed Mike. "Phil Redmond, the people's choice!"

The Still

The smells of summer were like a rich and overpowering perfume. As Mark cycled carefree along country roads, he could detect the sweet aroma of different plants and trees filling his nostrils. It was one of those summer days we fantasise about with its warm air, clear blue skies and the faint sounds of birds and bees all around. And then the smell changed. Suddenly Mark's nose was attacked by a very different, alien scent that he could not identify. It wasn't horrible but it wasn't sweet either. Baffled, he slowed down as if that would help him to work out what it was. Then it was gone and the previous smells returned.

Every summer would bring new challenges and one quandary everyone faced as pre-teen children was a mode of transport for the months of June, July and August. Too young to drive or own a motorbike, they had two choices: walk or ride a bicycle. It was all very well for children living in towns where their friends and the local shop were just around the corner. Where in the big estates there were areas of grass and, now and again, a play park. In the country areas it was much different. Friends lived along roads quite a distance away; some up long badly surfaced lanes leading to farm yards full of hostile poultry and animals of different sizes. The local shop was local only to those who lived around it; to the rest, it was half a mile away and for a pre-teen, it might as well have been in a different county. The council didn't build parks in the country but nature gave us trees with strong overhanging branches. A rope could be tied to one of them and there they had a swing.

But transport was a different story. There we faced limitations. There wasn't enough money to buy a bicycle to take us through the summer; so we improvised. There were a number of old bicycles lying about here and there, in and around our village, at any given time and the local garage owners were always willing to loan us a spanner or a screwdriver on condition that we brought them back on the same day. So, being ingenious because we had to be, we gathered up the bits and pieces of old bicycles until we had a heap of different objects including wheels, nuts, frames, handlebars and the very occasional set of brakes. These pieces of bicycles were then sorted out and all of the compatible bits were brought together and inspected. After much twisting, screwing and arguing, we found ourselves able to construct maybe three different bicycles. None of them had brakes or lights and the wheels could be somewhat buckled and devoid of mud guards but they could loosely be described as bicycles. We would prop them up against the nearest wall or hedge and congratulate ourselves and each other in what was no mean feat; bicycle production and a means of transport for each of us for the next three months.

The summer of 1976 looked promising. Weather forecasts predicted a scorching heatwave that would last forever, though Mark's granny swore she could predict the weather with far greater accuracy than any of the posh speaking men in suits. Although Mark accepted his granny's view on this, he was happy to believe the growing number of reports that all predicted a brilliant summer. By the beginning of June, the granny announced that the weather forecasters were correct, it would indeed be a great summer given the early blooms on certain flowers. Mark wondered if the forecasters were aware of this horticultural phenomenon before making their announcements and then decided they must have been or they wouldn't have been so confident in their predictions.

Mark was in a hurry to share his new found knowledge with his peers. Their grandparents never made predictions about anything, as far as he knew, so there was a bit of one-upmanship on his part. They met as usual by the Burn as arranged. As they sat listening to the gentle trickle of the clear water over the ancient stones, they looked out for stickleback fish and told each other of their plans for the months ahead. The more they planned, the more excited they became and the more excited they became, the more ridiculous their plans! They would make a rope swing. They would make three rope swings! They would make a fourth swing over the Burn so that if they fell off, they would land in the water! They sat speechless at the very thought of it, neglecting the fact that the Burn was only eight inches deep. They would hitch hike to Portrush! They would camp out all alone on the Forth nearby that was supposed to be haunted! They would build a raft from oil drums and float off down the River Bann and out to sea!

The more outlandish their plans became the more frightened they became at the thought of them. They terrified themselves and knew in their hearts they would not do what they talked about. But they couldn't let on, they each had to pretend that they would do each and every one of these things. Lost in thought at the prospect of summer, they didn't notice the arrival of a stranger.

"Well, what's happening?"

They looked to the source of the question and saw a well-fed youth of about their age peering over the bridge wall. His cheeks were flushed and chubby and his hair was gelled upwards but short. He fitted a bit too snugly into a white T-shirt and a navy tracksuit. They stared at him, unsure of how, or if, to answer his question.

"I'm Billy. Billy Watters. I will be staying down here with my granny for the next fortnight, so I will. Who are all you?"

They introduced themselves and eyed the new arrival with suspicion. His accent unknown to them but it certainly wasn't one they had heard before.

"Down here from where?" wee Al asked. They looked at Billy expectantly.

"Belfast, mate," he replied. "North Belfast to be exact."

I knew about Belfast. They had been advised at school that it was the capital city of Northern Ireland and Mrs White next door to Mark had spent time in a hospital there. It had been mentioned a lot on the news but never anything good.

But NORTH Belfast? What kind of a town has itself divided up into directions?

Wee Al was a step ahead of them here. His mother's sister had married a man from Belfast and moved there but he wasn't sure which direction of Belfast.

"What do you call her?" Billy asked and they waited with anticipation in the hope that Billy would know a relative of one of them.

"Madge Spence," wee Al replied hopefully.

Billy studied wee Al carefully and then shook his head. Wee Al seemed disappointed but shrugged his shoulders and looked at everyone in turn for a few seconds as if to ward off any challenges to his claim to have an aunt in Belfast.

"So, what do yous do around here?" Billy asked, glancing around the place with a look of despair.

"This and that," Mark replied, desperate not to sound boring but unwilling to admit the truth that there would be nothing much to do for a boy like Billy Watters.

Billy raised his eyebrows, half in doubt and half seeking some kind of clarification.

"I smelled that odd smell again down past McNaughtens," Mark ventured, hoping to invoke interest.

"I know that smell, it was there last year as well," Johnny Doherty yelled excitedly. "It's like nothing I ever smelled before. It definitely isn't human or anything to do with animals. It stays in your nose for ages too!"

"That's right!" Mark yelled back, delighted to have mentioned something that sounded interesting and had been corroborated by a third party.

"A 'smell'?" Billy retorted. "Like what?"

"Like nothing else in the world!" Johnny replied, proud to live in a place that had a scent unrivalled anywhere else on earth. That will show this Billy Watters, they thought collectively. They looked at him wide-eyed.

"Near the McNaughtens, you say," he replied mysteriously, looking into the distance. "That might be interesting. And who are these McNaughtens and where do they live?"

"Oh, you don't want to mess with the McNaughtens!" wee Al warned fearfully. "There are dozens of them at least and they hate wains! They will make you disappear if you go anywhere near them! Especially Billy McNaughten! He is fierce!"

"Wains? What's 'wains'?" Billy asked, truly baffled.

"It's what folk call children around here," Mark said gleefully. Not so smart now, Billy Watters! He thought as Billy seemed to consider the translation.

"And they hate wains, do they?" Billy asked no one in particular.

No one spoke. They were confused at this response. Surely wee Al's testimony would be enough for Billy Watters. There would be no way he would want to interfere with the McNaughtens after that! But they were wrong! All wee Al had done was whet Billy Watters' appetite for adventure!

"You still haven't told me where they live," Billy said accusingly. "Or are you too scared?"

Well! It was bad enough that this stranger had invaded their village with his strange way of talking and nosiness but to insinuate that they were cowards! That couldn't go unchallenged!

"Not a bit of us!" Mark shouted. "We just know all about them and they don't interest us. We don't bother them and they don't bother us. Anyway, it's time I had something to eat. I will see you boys later."

As if on cue, wee Al and Johnny claimed to be suffering from a similar hunger and needed to go home and receive food immediately. A bemused Billy Watters watched wordlessly as the three others went their separate ways for sustenance and sanctuary.

Undeterred, Billy walked along the quiet road seeking some kind of amusement. As he approached the centre of the village, he espied an elderly man standing against a lamp post and staring at the sky.

"Arite, mister!" Billy announced by way of greeting.

The old man looked at him suspiciously and then directed his gaze skywards again.

"Luks lake it's gan tae come doon," he said.

Billy looked at him quizzically. He had no idea what the old man had just said but assumed it was related to the sky so he looked up to where the old man was staring. All he could see was grey clouds passing over the sun.

"Looks like it might rain, mister," he offered.

The old man looked at him contemptuously and tutted loudly. Billy had the feeling he had offended the old man in some way but couldn't imagine how.

"I am looking to know where the McNaughtens live, so I am," he said slowly. The old man was obviously a foreigner and it was just Billy's luck to find someone in this backwater place to talk to and then discover his companion obviously couldn't speak or understand English!

"The McNaughtens, ye say? A wudnae be botherin them if a was ye. They dinnae tak ower kinely tae yins botherin them."

Billy was completely baffled. Had the old man told him where the McNaughtens live? Had he given Billy directions? Billy pointed his finger down a road to their left.

"Down that way, mister?" he asked.

"Heth aye an fer aal their days tae," the old man replied nodding.

Billy nodded believing that to be the best response to this strange man and his strange speech, and set off down the country road, pulling blades of grass from the ditches and swishing them aimlessly as he walked. He was startled by a sudden noise from behind the hedge and his heart skipped a beat as he heard an awesome pounding sound coming from that direction. Gingerly he peered over the bushes and was shocked to find himself confronted by a cow, or maybe a bull or some kind of bovine. The animal stared at him for a moment and then emitted a loud noise which actually startled the unsuspecting townie. He jumped off the ditch and jogged along the road, checking for gaps in the hedge through which that beast might emerge. As he ran, looking behind himself every few seconds, he was struck by the presence of a very peculiar smell in his nostrils. He stopped suddenly, forgetting about the brown and white mooing monster behind the hedge a hundred metres back and inhaled deeply through his nose. What on earth was that? The boys had been right; this was a singularly unique smell, neither pleasant nor noxious and totally indescribable. He tried to think of other scents and aromas he had experienced in his life but there was no comparison to this. Slowly he followed the aroma and quickly saw a small cottage tucked in behind a wild hedge. The hedge hid a once-neat lawn that would now keep that cow thing fed for a month. Billy Watters had never seen grass as tall as this unless on TV. The cottage looked deserted with badly hung net curtains trying desperately to hide whatever was inside the house. Billy stood and stared, mystified by the smell and knowing it was definitely coming from this house.

Suddenly the front door of the house flew open and Billy was confronted by something that had some but not all of the appearances of a human. The creature had hair as wild as the hedge and garden and a collarless shirt that only partially covered once-white long johns. The animal had no teeth but it's eyes blazed with fury and from the toothless gums came roars of incoherent rage! Billy Watters was dumbstruck and frozen with shock. He couldn't move a millimetre as the creature stomped barefoot across the mixture of stones and grass towards him, flailing its arms wildly and spit discharging from its lips like bullets.

Suddenly Billy realised the creature was only a couple of metres from him and he came to his senses. In a swift movement, Billy spun around and ran. He ran faster than he had ever run in his entire life, not daring to look behind him once. He passed the brown and white animal looking through the hedge and didn't give it a thought. It didn't matter to Billy Watters if that was a cow or a bull or a bullock; it wasn't half as frightening as the roaring menace behind him. It was only when he ran out of breath that he stopped and looked behind him. To his relief, Billy saw only an empty road. He had outrun the creature and, between gasps, he prayed a brief prayer of thanks for having survived the whole terrifying experience. As he resumed his journey back to the village at a much slower pace, Billy reflected on the dangers of the countryside. He thought it was bad in Belfast but not in all the years he had lived there (which was all his life) had he been terrorised like that! As he approached the centre of the village, he saw the old man still standing there looking from the sky to the ground. The old man paused for a moment and looked at Billy who, red faced and sweating, passed him by.

"Ye fun the McNaughtens then, a see, judgin by the luk o ye," the old man observed.

Again, Billy was clueless and opted not to respond, walking on towards his grandmother's house. He had heard the old man saying 'McNaughtens' though. Maybe he had tried to warn him but as Billy didn't speak his language, he hadn't understood. Glancing back, he noticed the old man looking after him chuckling and shaking his head.

What a weird place this is! Billy thought.

The next day, Billy waited about the centre of the village hoping to see the boys he had met the previous day. He had spent the previous evening considering everything they had said about the McNaughtens and compared all that with his own brief experience. He had concurred that the local boys had not, in fact, been exaggerating. The McNaughtens were a very distinct and worrying species.

"Hi Billy!" wee Al shouted from somewhere, causing Billy to jump. "What's wrong with you? Have you bad nerves or something?"

"No, I have not!" Billy retorted defensively. "I just didn't see you, so I didn't. Where's the rest of them?"

"Over there," wee Al replied pointing at Mark and Johnny as they plodded along in the heat.

They returned to their spot near the Burn and chatted idly though all of them noticed a change in Billy. He wasn't the same chatty boy he had been yesterday. There was nothing too impressive about him now. But what had happened? Billy Watters had hardly spoken a single word.

"I went to the McNaughtens yesterday," Billy said suddenly. The others looked at him with a mixture of amazement and disbelief. This admission explained the change in Billy

Watters but was he telling the truth. He seemed psychologically impaired, yes, but there were no visible scars. Surely no one ever went to the McNaughtens uninvited and left there without some kind of physical disfigurement!

"Are you telling the truth?" Johnny asked, almost in a whisper.

"Aye, I am," Billy Watters answered, looking at each of them challengingly. "I saw the madman himself, too!"

"No way!" exclaimed wee Al. "You never saw Billy McNaughten up close and lived! I have never heard of anyone doing that!"

"It was shocking, so it was!" Billy Watters explained. "There I was just out for a walk and I smelt that smell you were all chatting about yesterday. I followed the scent of it and came to a wee cottage with a wild garden and a hedge that was growing every shape." The others looked at each other wide eyed and nodded; this described the McNaughten house perfectly so Billy Watters must be telling the truth!

"Anyway, I had a stick in my hand for swishing the grass and the hedges and before I knew it, I was in front of that cottage, so I was. Well, looking at it, I wasn't even sure if anyone still lived in it. It was in that bad shape I thought it was a derelict building."

Billy paused to read the reactions of his audience. They were staring at him open-mouthed and in awe of this new found friend from that Belfast. They were waiting on his every word. Now would be a good time to exaggerate, Billy thought slyly.

"Well, being not one who scares easy, I tried to open the gate but it was seised. So, not one to give up, I climbed over the gate and into the yard."

"You did not!" wee Al explained in total horror. "The McNaughtens yard! All by yourself!"

"Certainly!" Billy retorted full of pride. "Well, I still had my stick and I went to walk along the side of the house to go round the back and just as I was a metre from the house, the door flew open and there he was! Billy McNaughten!"

"No way!" shouted Mark, unable to believe what he was hearing. "So, what was he wearing?"

The others nodded at each other approvingly. Billy McNaughten had worn the same clothes every day for as long as anyone could remember. It was said by the older boys that he bathed only when there was a full moon and even then it was in the Burn amongst the frogs and sticklebacks.

"He wore a short with no collar and in below it some kind of vest, only it had buttons. It had maybe been white at one time but not when I saw it. It was between white and grey. He had on grey trousers that looked like they were part of a suit at one time and he had on wellington boots; green ones."

By now the others were beside themselves! This is exactly how Billy McNaughten dressed! Only Mark needed a little more convincing.

"What did he look like? His face I mean."

"Ah well, it wasn't a face I could ever forget!" Billy said dramatically. "He had the widest head of grey hair, sticking out everywhere. It had never ever seen a comb in its life! He had no teeth at all and instead of saying actual words, he just made terrible noises that sounded as if they 'should' be words. His eyes were red and like a vampire! He looked like someone had made him in a garage somewhere!"

The boys all looked at each other with a mixture of shock and horror. There was no doubt about it – Billy Watters had supplied far too much information and detail to be lying!

"Anyway, that smell; I think we need to investigate it. Is there a field to the back of the McNaughtens we could use to get close without them seeing us?"

"Are you sure that's wise, Billy?" wee Al asked, his eyes wide with terror at the very prospect of it. "I mean, if they see us, that's it! We are dead!"

"Right boys, seriously," Billy began thoughtfully. "How many people have you actually known to have come into contact with the McNaughtens and actually disappeared? Like, name five!"

The boys looked at Billy Watters open mouthed but silent. Each of them tried hard to recall someone, anyone, who might have fallen victim to the McNaughtens. However, after a few minutes of frantic thought, they were shocked to admit even to themselves that they couldn't think of a single person! This distressed them because everyone knew folk disappeared in that garden and house. Didn't they? Suddenly the boys weren't so certain. Silently they racked their brains trying to think of someone, anyone, who had disappeared at the hands of the McNaughtens. They couldn't think of a single person!

"Aye, thought as much, so I did," Billy Watters said triumphantly. "It's all talk and nonsense to keep us young ones away from them. They're at something and older folk tell us fairy tales to keep us from finding out the truth!"

This was a thought-provoking theory. The boys thought about this and concurred that Billy Watters might actually be right! This was all a ruse! They had been tricked by older folk and their wild tales. Now they were determined to find out what the McNaughtens were up to and what was the source of that strange smell.

"There is a field at the back of their house, right enough," said Mark suddenly. "We can get into the field through a gate a right bit away from the McNaughtens."

"That's right!" exclaimed Johnny, "and if we crawl along the hedge, we will be able to spy on them through the hedge and see what this is all about!"

Everyone nodded except wee Al who looked fearful and stared at the ground to avoid eye contact with the others.

"Right, no time like the present!" Billy said, jumping up. "Let's get into that field and end this mystery!"

As they walked down the road towards the gate, the other boys couldn't help but think that Billy Watters wasn't above sarcasm.

The field seemed to go on forever. Even Billy Watters seemed impressed! The perimeter hedge seemed to be miles away from the gate as they slowly walked towards the hedge at the back of the McNaughten's home. As they neared the spot, they stopped suddenly when they heard outbursts of incoherent ramblings. Although the boys did not know what was being said, they could tell it was being said in anger, if not fury. The strange smell grew stronger as they dropped to their knees and crawled along towards the hedge at the McNaughtens. Gingerly they peeked through gaps in the hedge and looked on as a younger member of the clan gesticulated wildly at Billy McNaughten who responded with even wilder gestures and noisy outbursts from a toothless mouth. Then an ancient woman, who looked to be around a thousand years old, came hobbling out of the house yelling at the two men. After another crazed exchange, the three of them disappeared into the house.

"Right boys, this is it!" Billy Watters hissed. "Are we going in to see what the smell is about or what?"

Wee Al looked as if he was about to die with fright. He felt his short legs go weak and tremble at the very thought of it. Johnny swallowed hard and never took his eyes off the back door of the house. Mark stared at Billy Watters as if the latter had gone mad.

"It's broad daylight!" Mark hissed as loudly as he dared. "What if they see us?"

"And what if they do?" Billy countered. "There's just that gummy old man and an ancient old woman and that other boy who looks like he never fought anything more than boredom in his whole life! There's four of us and we're young and fit. Come on!"

Despite themselves and their nervous anxiety, the three locals followed Billy Watters through a hole in the hedge into a wilderness of a garden. Old wire fences lay half covered with grass and parts of various types of machinery lay rusting here and there. The smell was by now overpowering and the quest to discover the source of it soon overcame their irrational fear of the McNaughtens. Slowly they crept through the grass, avoiding random iron and rusted steel impediments. They scrambled over fallen fencing and Mark had to bite his hand to avoid screaming as a vicious nail tore his skin. As they reached a dilapidated wooden shed, they paused. A strange noise was coming from within the rotting boards that served as the shed wall, accompanied with the pungent odour that brought them here in the first place. Billy Watters half stood and peered in the open door. He stared inside for a moment before turning to his friends and giving them a puzzled look. He beckoned them over and in less than a minute, all four were crammed into the shed staring at the strangest contraption they had ever seen.

Before them stood an assortment of different things, all connected in different ways. There was a steel boiler which appeared to be full of some kind of liquid but it was sitting on top of four wooden pallets so the boys couldn't see inside it. Coming from it was a length of copper piping that curled along the way to a small old-fashioned bath. A clear liquid was dripping out of the copper pipe into the bath and the smell was really overpowering. As well as the strange liquid, there was a smell of burning plastic somewhere that was really nauseous. Billy Watters moved around the side of the boiler and gasped. He turned to the others and they squeezed past him to have a look. And there was the source of the burning plastic: a single socket had two old fashioned double adapters plugged into each other and rammed in to the source. Leads of various widths and colours ran from the double adapters, one serving the boiler, another a smaller boiler at the back which bubbled noisily and a third was attached to a radio from whence came nothing but static. There was also a kettle plugged in and something else the boys did not recognise.

"It's overloaded!" Mark exclaimed as the sharp smell of melting plastic competed with the liquid to give off the most horrendous stench.

"I think we should go!" wee Al hissed only just above the noise of the bubbling boilers and radio static.

Johnny nodded in agreement as he continued to stare worriedly at the overloaded socket and then to the boilers and back again.

"WHAT ARE YOU LOT DOING IN THERE!" a voice roared from behind them. It was another of the McNaughtens and he was dressed in a boiler suit with hands caked in some kind of oil. Before the boys could react, Billy McNaughten appeared behind the younger one, his wild hair flying about and his eyes blazing in anger. Awful sounds came flowing from his toothless mouth, terrifying everyone, including Billy Watters! Wee Al was the first to make a move, diving in between the legs of the young McNaughten and scrambling between the wellington boots of an increasingly hysterical Billy. The latter swatted and swiped, his arms flailing in a bid to catch wee Al who squealed in terror as he scrambled to his feet and ran off down the garden. Mark and Johnny took advantage of the melee and ran straight for the younger McNaughten, crashing into him and sending him reeling into Billy who lost his balance and fell. The boys jumped over the tangle of McNaughtens and ran after wee Al, squealing just as loudly. Billy Watters left it too late to escape by the door because just as he was about to make a run for it, the younger McNaughten was on his feet, arms spread and ready to grab whoever came out next. Spotting the risk, Billy Watters looked frantically around him and his eye caught a couple of particularly rotten boards on the wall nearest him. Without a moment's hesitation, he charged at the wall and with a crash, he ran straight through the boards as the splinters scattered behind him. Up ahead he saw wee Al tangled in wire and the other two trying desperately to free him because by now, the two McNaughtens were on their feet and the old crone was out yelling at Billy who was roaring at the younger McNaughten who was shouting at the three hapless friends and Billy Watters. Suddenly, wee Al was torn free from the tangle of wire, minus his shoe and the four of them sprinted to the hedge with the two male McNaughtens still shouting and throwing peat turf at them. The old witch was exhausted by all the excitement and had resorted to sitting on the door step mumbling and shaking her head.

The four boys crashed through the hedge simultaneously and landed in the field in different shapes. They got up together and ran for their lives, fearing to glance back in case the McNaughtens were behind them. Wee Al lagged behind, both on account of his short legs but also due to his lost shoe. After about five minutes, Johnny flopped down on the grass, quickly followed by Mark, Billy Watters and eventually, wee Al. All four felt as if their lungs would burst!

"Did you see the face of Billy McNaughten?" Mark gasped. "We might not know of anyone he has killed but he's a killer all right!"

"Aye, right enough," Billy Watters replied. "He's a mad man so he is! Did you see me, though? Did you see how I burst through that wall like the Incredible Hulk?"

Everyone nodded breathlessly and they lay back in the grass reliving and retelling the account of what happened to them. As always, with the telling, their accounts quickly became detached from reality. In the end they gave up talking and just lay quietly, lost in their own thoughts. Suddenly wee Al piped up.

"The only thing is, they have my shoe! If the police comes, they can use it to identify me!"

"Aye, right enough!" Billy Watters shouted, sitting bolt upright. "You have to get rid of the other one so if they do find your shoe, they will have nothing to match it with!"

The other two agreed. Billy Watters was from Belfast, after all, so they would know these things. They got up and walked to the shallow Burn and stood solemnly as wee Al took his remaining shoe off and carefully placed it in the water. They watched in silent tribute as the lone item of footwear was carried downstream. They then decided to call it a day and go to their respective homes and mention nothing about any of this to their families.

Early next morning, Mark awoke early, hearing much laughter and loud discourses in the kitchen. He joined his parents and asked what all the fuss was about.

"The McNaughtens!" his dad replied and Mark's heart skipped a beat.

"What about them?" he asked tentatively.

"Well, they are in some form the day! Last night, something happened in one of their shacks out the back and it went on fire. And that's not the best of it! The fire set off their still and the whole thing blew up and burnt the shed and the one next to it to the ground! The second shed had dry peats in it and apparently it was like a war zone!" His dad laughed heartily. "I can just see that Billy boy and his old mother out trying to save the still! Not to mention all the other ones that live there from time to time!"

Mark could hardly believe his ears! He knew straight away how the fire started!

"It was an overload! Their plugs were all overloaded. That's what Billy Watters said and he's from Belfast! We smelled the burning plastic yester..." he stopped suddenly, realising what he had said. His parents looked at him accusingly.

"I mean, Billy Watters smelled it and told us about it!"

His parents looked unconvinced but then reverted back to their speculations on the reactions of the McNaughten clan at the loss of their illicit income and their winter fuel. After a hasty breakfast, Mark set off to meet his friends and within the hour they were all together, beside the Burn. They also speculated wildly about how Billy McNaughten would have reacted but with more passion than Mark's parents. Maybe Billy had killed the younger McNaughten? Maybe the old witch had cast spells on them? Maybe she had cast a spell on the shed causing it to burn down? Maybe the McNaughtens would blame them! The latter was too awful to contemplate and although they would have loved to have cycled past the McNaughtens to see the damage for themselves, they were too afraid to do so.

Billy Watters returned to his home in Belfast a few days later. The three boys gathered to wave goodbye to their friend and watch him drive off. They only ever saw him a few times after that when he came down to visit his relatives but he only ever stayed a day or a few hours. After a few years he stopped coming down but the friends took comfort from believing that somewhere in the world, Billy Watters was alive and well and remembering them and the time they spent together.

None of the boys ever troubled the McNaughtens again. And none of them ever made a still.

The Holiday

Maud Watters took another sip of her tea and sighed audibly. Her son was spending yet another day upstairs in his room and there was nothing Maud could do about it. This had been going on for far too long and the more she thought about it, the more she blamed herself for his behaviour. From his earliest days, Alfie had the wildest imagination she had ever known. At school, his P6 teacher had asked her class to write a story of their choosing. The next day, the class submitted their stories, all of them one side of a page, the writing large. Alfie had offered six pages of small writing, both sides of each page filled. The teacher had spoken to Maud about it and whilst overwhelmed at the size of the story, she was concerned at the content. It had been a wild fantasy that made no real sense, jumping from one theme to another with no correlation throughout. A bit like his life, Maud mused. Anyway, she felt she had a solution to her son's solitude, glancing at the envelope she was fingering nervously. Once I have my tea, I will give it to him, she decided, before pouring herself another cup as if to postpone the inevitable.

Meanwhile, in his bedroom with the curtains drawn and a spotlight beaming down from the ceiling, Alfie Watters was engaging in his happiest past time. He had put a red lightbulb into the spotlight and now the room was bathed in a dull red glow. Alfie stood opposite a full-length mirror and looked closely at himself. He was a rock star and his public loved him. For hours at a time he stood in front of this mirror and sang to his reflection as the hi-fi speakers blasted his favourite songs. At the end of each song, Alfie demonstrated his appreciation of the imaginary screaming crowd by bowing and shouting 'Thank you!' at his reflection. For years he had played air guitar as he sang but one day his mother had entered the room unexpectedly and caught him halfway through Parisienne Walkways. The light from the hall that entered the room as the door opened caught his eye so Alfie, embarrassed and uncomfortable, let on he had pins and needles in his hands and told his mother that although it may have looked like he had been playing air guitar, he was really only trying to get the feeling back in his fingers. His mother had simply set his tea down on the dressing table, nodded and left.

The next day, Alfie had gone along to the nearest sports shop. He enquired about a cheap tennis racquet but the shop assistant had tried to trick him into buying an expensive one. Alfie had recognised the ruse and stood his ground. A 'cheap' one he had reiterated, or he would take his custom elsewhere. The girl had acquiesced but not before trying to convince him to purchase a T-shirt and shorts. Alfie was too clever for her though and quickly paid for the racquet and ran out of the shop while the girl was in the back looking for the sportswear. As he walked down the street, Alfie congratulated himself on his quick-witted response. Shops were dark and dangerous places where highly trained confidence tricksters flattered and conned members of the public into buying loads of things they didn't even want. But they would need to get up earlier to beat Alfie Watters! He had their number, he thought smugly.

When he got home, he slid the tennis racquet up below his jacket. He didn't want his mother seeing it and getting the wrong idea because Maud was obsessive. If she saw the racquet, she would assume that Alfie had taken an interest in sports and then she would be asking him every day if he was going to play a game and he couldn't be bothered with that. In his room, he quickly removed the racquet, slipped off his jacket and adopted his superstar pose in front of the mirror. Flicking on the hi-fi, Alfie gave his reflection a bow and began a muted rendition of 'All Night Long', head banging his bald cranium furiously. He strummed the tennis racquet furiously as he pretended to sing and lost himself to his imaginary audience. When the song finished, Alfie looked at the tennis racquet both real and the one in the mirror and decided it was a very wise purchase. No sooner had he concurred this point than the next song began and off he went again.

Maud decided that she had waited long enough. She was determined to get her son out of that room no matter what! Stuffing the envelope in her dressing gown pocket, she climbed the stairs and headed for Alfie's bedroom. She had been wrong to sell the caravan to the Pam, she conceded. It had worried her how much time her Alfie had spent in it with his computer and all that music and games but at least it had given him somewhere to go. She hesitated at the door of his room and decided to knock loudly before entering.

"Alfie, could you turn that music down a wee bit, please," she began. "I have something to say to you."

Alfie looked stunned to see his mother standing there looking so serious. He quickly killed the blasting music with one press of the remote control and sat on his bed looking questioningly at Maud.

"I know we have been through all this before, son," Maud said haltingly, as if not sure how to proceed with this conversation. "I really believe it isn't healthy, you spending so much time up here in your room. Anyway, I feel guilty for selling the caravan as I know it was like a wee refuge for you. So, here's what it is, son. I took some of that money I was paid for the caravan and I went to the travel agent and bought you a really special birthday present. You will be thirty years old in a few days so I thought you might want to spend it somewhere nice."

Here she produced the tattered envelope and reached it to Alfie who grasped it from her.

"I have bought you an all-inclusive holiday in Spain. You won't have to spend any of your own money unless you want to. The flight, transfer and accommodation are all paid for as well as your meals and whatever you drink. There! That's it. What do you think?"

Alfie looked at the ticket he had removed from the envelope. It was true! He was going on a holiday to Spain! He looked at his mother, then his reflection in the mirror and then back to the ticket. Immediately his wild imagination kicked in. His plane could be hijacked and he might well save the day by overpowering the terrorists single-handedly! His hotel might catch fire and he would save an old lady on the second floor! A child might get into difficulties swimming and he would dive in and save the poor infant! The possibilities were limitless—especially if you were Alfie Watters!

Alfie was beside himself with excitement and jumped up and hugged his mother. Maud was surprised at this reaction and didn't know how to respond. He thanked her repeatedly and flung open the curtains, switching off the red light and made his bed. In two days, he would be on his way to Spain. Seeing his tennis racquet lying on the floor, he suddenly felt embarrassed by it and kicked it under the bed. No need for that for a while, he thought happily. I will sing every night in that Spain. I will sing songs I am familiar with and that way, if a record scout or a band manager happens to hear him, he could come back to Northern Ireland with a record deal! Unable to contain himself, Alfie went straight to the attic to retrieve a little used suitcase he knew to be up there somewhere. It was time to pack and to give careful consideration to what clothes he would be taking. Appearances are everything, he decided, especially in terms of attracting a girl as well as a record company. The next two days would have his over active imagination going far beyond all previous madness as he pictured himself giving it large in Spain. Beware gringos' because Alfie Watters is on his way, he thought smiling. Staring at his reflection, he gave a thumbs up and laughed loudly with joy.

Despite the fact that his plane did not get hijacked, Alfie had an enjoyable flight. He exhausted himself speculating about the careers and darkest secrets of the other passengers before falling asleep for the remaining hour of the flight. When travelling in the bus taking him and other guests to the hotel, he was struck with a fear that the bus driver may be a terrorist taking them all to a desolate place where they would be held hostage until ransoms were paid. Worriedly, he wondered how much of the caravan money his mother still had in case that did happen. As it turned out, the driver was pleasant and helpful and kindly dropped them all off at the correct hotel without incident. Alfie was relieved and disappointed but convinced himself that adventure lay just around the corner. After checking in and inspecting his room, Alfie applied factor to his almost luminous white skin and headed to the pool. There were quite a few about so Alfie sucked in his belly, adjusted his sunglasses and skirted the edge of the pool in search of a sunbed. Had he been paying less attention to a group of boisterous young women and more to where he was walking, he might have noticed the pools of water. As it was, he didn't and he slipped and skidded his bare feet along the edge before eventually falling in headlong into the pool. For someone who fantasised about saving an infant, Alfie couldn't actually swim so when he went beneath the water, his mouth wide open in shock, he swallowed what felt like half the pool water and went into panic overdrive. Bubbles spewed out of his mouth as his feet hit the bottom and Alfie believed he was about to die. Suddenly a hand grabbed his up stretched arm and he was being pulled to the surface. His saviour managed to get him completely out of the water and lay him on his side as the water spurted from Alfie's mouth every time he coughed.

"Are you OK, mate?" the saviour asked.

Alfie sat up shakily, his sunglasses sitting at a curious angle on his face. Quickly he adjusted his glasses to perch on his nose but the lenses were splattered with water and his eyes were blurred so he couldn't really see the man who had just saved him.

"Aye, I am dead on," Alfie began, his mind racing. "There was a kid in the pool and he looked as if he was in trouble so I just dived in but I took cramp after I got him to safety and that's when you came along!"

The stranger treated this with scepticism as he had been handing out cards for his bar/restaurant along the side of the pool and had noticed this chubby lad slipping and falling headlong into the pool. Thinking Alfie was in shock, the stranger let it go.

"That's a Northern Ireland accent," said the stranger. "I am from there myself but I live here now and I have a wee business in town. Here, take a card and pop in and see me, sure. Karaoke every night from 7 pm to late!"

At that, the stranger left and immediately Alfie forgot about his humiliating fall. Karaoke? Well, that boy is in for a treat! Alfie decided there and then that he would indeed visit this establishment and show a few people how to sing. Tonight, he mused, you will be witnesses to the Alfie Watters Show! He then got up and squelched his way back to the room. It was 4:30 pm so he needed to shower, grab a quick snack and get down to this place good and early for a seat at the front. Tonight, Alfie, you will be...whoever you want to be! He laughed with glee at the very thought of the evening ahead.

In the Olympic, John Spence polished the counter and looked around his establishment with renewed satisfaction. He reckoned that the cards he had distributed that day would result in a huge upturn in trade. The bar was well stocked in eager readiness and the tables shone, waiting to be overburdened with drinks. John glanced at the cash register, wondering would it ever be able to cope with the amount of money that would be thrust into its trays this evening. Moving here was the best decision he had ever made! This was his first tourist season but he had been assured that if he put in the hours during summer, he could take it very easy during the winter months. In fact, he might even return to Belfast and stay with his parents for a few weeks. Maybe even a month?

John sighed as he looked at the early customers. A demure blond lady sat alone sipping a cocktail, her face hid behind a pair of massive sunglasses. Although they obscured most of her face, she seemed like a good-looking woman but around 40 years old John estimated so too old for him. To his left, his parents sat quietly. He had invited them over for a fortnight and was surprised when they accepted. They used to caravan but a bad experience had put paid to that. He noted that his father seemed happy, sitting there people watching, occasionally looking up at the sky outside. Likely looking for pigeons,

John decided, as that particular species of bird had held a life-long fascination for John's dad. His mother never changed. She sat looking glum, staring straight ahead. It was hard to know if she was happy but then it had always been that way. She seemed happiest being unhappy. She must be delirious then, John thought wryly, as she always looks unhappy. He sniggered at his thoughts and went about getting things ready.

Joan Grace sipped her cocktail with her normal reserve. No gulping it down or lining them up for Joan. She was enjoying herself in her own quiet way and when she saw the blackboard for the Olympic on the pavement advertising an ulster fry, she didn't hesitate to enter the building for a wee taste of home. She had had her traumas back home with the breakdown of her marriage and then being held up by a would-be robber in the post office where she worked. If anyone deserved a break, it was her and she was making the most of it. She used the shield of her sunglasses to hide the fact that she was studying the middle-aged couple across the room. The woman looked angry but the man seemed pleasant enough. They must be married a long time, she mused, judging by the lack of conversation between them. Now and again, she glanced at the barman. There was something familiar about him but she couldn't put her finger on it. Maybe his bleached hair had been a different colour and the moustache could have been grown lately. His accent was Northern Ireland and Belfast in particular. Maybe that was it? Could it be that he just seemed familiar because he had a familiar accent? She thought about it a while longer and then decided to just enjoy the music coming from the jukebox.

Madge Spence had been surprised when her son announced that he was leaving Belfast for a new life in Spain. Her John? He had hardly ever travelled outside Belfast yet there he was moving to another country? She had tried to dissuade him by reminding him that he couldn't even boil an egg but John had countered that he didn't like eggs so that wouldn't be a problem. She told him the sun irritated his skin but John said he wouldn't spend a lot of time in the sun as he would be too busy making a fortune. Well, it was his money, she begrudgingly accepted. He had two claims, one as a victim of a robbery where he apparently foiled the attempt by restraining the armed robber and another as a hit-and-run victim during his short career as a policeman. He had never said how much he had received but he had, in fairness, bought his father a new pigeon loft and treated her to a makeover and new outfit. When they got the call to come over and stay a week with him in his apartment above his bar/ restaurant, her husband had simply smiled. It was left to Madge to pack, organise a taxi to the airport and buy sun lotions. John had very kindly paid for the return flight so all they needed was spending money and as all the food and drink in the Olympic was free, it would be a nice cheap break.

Alfie Watters strode purposefully along the sun-baked streets on his way to the Olympic. He was covered in sun oil and sprayed from head to toe with deodorant. A strong aftershave had been applied to his smooth face and as he passed people, they tended to stop and stare. The real cause was the overpowering scents emanating from Alfie but he decided that his handsome good looks were the cause. In no time at all, Alfie espied The Olympic, probably the most misnamed place in all of Spain for there was nothing 'Olympic' about it. Alfie glanced quickly inside and then studied the blackboard for information. And there it was; the magic word! Karaoke. He checked the start time and then his watch and realised he had over an hour to wait. Well, he thought, I might as well wait inside.

The barman was the chap who had given Alfie the card at the pool. When Alfie ordered his drink, the barman didn't seem to recognise him. Taking a sip of his drink, he became annoyed at this lack of recognition.

"Not know me, mate?" he asked the barman. "I am the one from the pool earlier today, the one who nearly drowned saving the kid. Remember you helped me out of the water?"

John laughed loudly. That wasn't how he remembered it at all but this character was a paying customer so if that's what he says happened, then so be it.

"That's right! I am laughing because I didn't recognise you without the shades and in dry clothes," he lied. "Come to think of it, you do look familiar, very familiar in fact. What part of Belfast are you from?"

"Oh, I have lived here and there," Alfie said mysteriously. "I have had quite a few jobs and they meant I had to move about. Between us, I do work for the security forces and I mean at the highest level! I have been on active service in many countries and I have seen some things, believe me!"

John looked hard at this man who had just admitted to being a spy. Was he crazy?

"Also, I have seen some things back in Belfast, if you know what I mean? Like, violence and the like. I was almost shot one time!"

"Seriously?" John asked doubtfully. "Well, Belfast can be like that I suppose."

"Yeah, mate," Alfie said slowly, looking far into the distance as if reliving some terrible experience. "I was an innocent bystander that day. I called into a post office and suddenly an armed man burst into the place to rob it! Well, I was just about to pounce on him when another guy rammed the robber and knocked him on his back! I knew the other guy had the robber subdued so I immediately looked to the other customers to ensure their safety. An elderly lady was on the ground, the cashier was on the ground and, of course, the robber was on the ground with the other chap on top of him! It was unbelievable! Fair play to that boy! He fixed the robber good and proper!"

Suddenly it dawned on John; this was the one and only Alfie Watters! Before him stood the greatest fantasist in all Belfast, the man known as an exaggerating spoofer who couldn't tell the truth no matter how hard he tried. Alfie Watters! Did he not know who he was talking about? He, John Spence, owner of the Olympic, was the hero who subdued the robber! It hadn't happened remotely like Alfie remembered it but the variations from the truth were nothing to do with the passing of time. John was half concussed that day and wasn't too sure of what happened himself but he was confident that it wasn't as Alfie described. Even on the day it happened, when Alfie gave his witness testimony, it was nothing like what had really happened. Still, Alfie's account had made John a hero. In fact, Alfie's account had changed John's entire life!

"That was me!" John exclaimed, though Alfie looked doubtful. "Imagine my hair the colour it was and no moustache! It was me! I foiled the robbery that day! I don't believe it! You're Alfie Watters who made the statement to the police!"

Alfie looked dumbstruck. It was this barman indeed! As the dawn of realisation rested on Alfie, John shouted past him to the middle-aged couple.

"Look, ma! It's Alfie Watters from Belfast! Do you remember him, da?"

Madge looked shocked and nodded slowly. Alfie Watters, the Walter Mitty of Belfast! She remembered him as a young boy running around spreading his lies and wild stories. What an idiot! And here he was!

"I know exactly who he is, John. This is the man who made you a hero during that post office robbery! Well, well! Alfie Watters!"

Suddenly the quiet and demure lady sitting alone removed her sunglasses and looked at John, then Alfie and then Madge and her husband.

"I don't believe it!" she exclaimed. "I was the teller that day!"

Everyone turned and looked at the woman. John, whose recollection of that incident was hazy, couldn't be sure and Madge wasn't there so she, for once, couldn't comment. But not so Alfie Watters. Staring at the woman, he remembered her being spoken to softly by the policeman. He remembered her being taken shaken and upset by the arm, past him as he told his story of what had happened. It was her!

"That's right!" Alfie shouted excitedly. "You're Jean or Jane or something!"

The blond woman nodded vigorously and corrected Alfie. "Yes, well, it's Joan actually but close enough!"

It was a small world indeed! What were the chances of this group of people meeting up again, especially in a bar in Spain of all places! Alfie went straight to her table, advising John to bring her whatever she was drinking and inviting John's parents to join them. Madge and her husband made their way across the floor, more bemused than anything else at the way things had turned out. John brought fresh drinks and joined them for a few before the crowds gathered.

For the next week, the five met daily and spent many hours together. Madge managed to surprise herself and everyone else by abandoning her usual sarcasm and innate rage and became the life and soul of their meetings. Even her reticent husband joined in and uttered full sentences, sometimes initiating conversations as opposed to simply answering questions as briefly as possible. John did notice something of a bond forming between Alfie and Joan Grace and when he was out at the shops in the mornings, he would see them walking together or in outdoor cafes. John was happy! His mother had remembered how to have fun, his father had the ability to speak unprompted and Alfie and Joan seemed to be hitting it off. John was pleased and grateful for all of this and laughed as he thought back to that day in the post office. How things had changed!

On the last day of their holidays, the Spences, Alfie and Joan called with John to say goodbye. They all promised to keep in touch and meet up back in Belfast with John agreeing readily to meet up whenever he came back home. Alfie announced that Joan had agreed to see him regularly as more than a friend and they all had one last drink to toast the happy, albeit unlikely, couple.

As the holiday makers left, John waved and watched the taxi until it was out of sight.

And then he laughed.

What a week! What an outcome! Isn't life strange?